Slaves of the Blood Wolves

I0458213

Weird Menace #5

SLAVES OF THE BLOOD WOLVES - WEIRD MENACE CLASSICS # 5
$5.50 per copy

Edited and published by Robert Weinberg 10606 S. Centra
Park, Chicago, Il. 60655

ACKNOWLEDGMENTS

SLAVES OF THE BLOOD WOLVES by Arthur J. Burks,
copyright © 1935 by Popular Publications for
Terror Tales, December 1935. Copyright renewed
1963. Reprinted by permission of Mrs. Ruth
Burks.

SATAN SENDS A WOMAN by Wyatt Blassingame,
copyright © 1936 by Popular Publications
for Terror Tales, January 1936. Copyright
renewed 1964. Reprinted by permission of
the author's agent, Blassingame, McCauley
and Wood.

THE RED EYE OF RIN-PO-CHE by Norvell W. Page,
copyright © 1939 by Popular Publications for
Dime Mystery, November 1939. Copyright renewed
1967. Reprinted by permission of Mrs. Gean C.
Purcell and Mrs. Natalie Beattie.

GIRL OF THE GOAT GOD by Arthur Leo Zagat,
copyright © 1935 by Popular Publications
for Dime Mystery, November 1935. Copyright
renewed 1963. Reprinted by permission of
Mrs. Ruth Zagat.
Cover by Steve Fabian

FIRST EDITION

WILDSIDE PRESS

CONTENTS

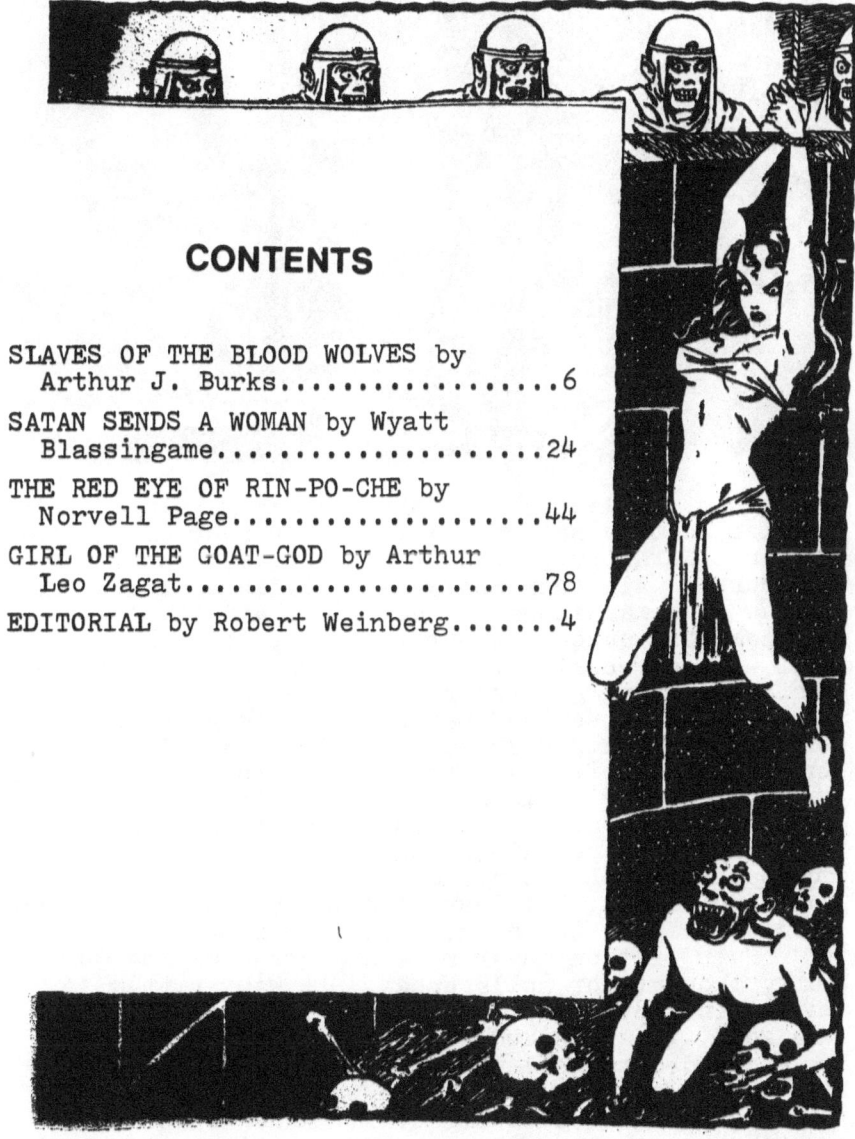

Our latest collection of Weird-Menace reprints features
an excellent selection of stories by four of the top
writers in the pulp field - Blassingame, Page, Zagat
and Burks. All four men were prolific contributors
to the pulp magazines of the 1930's and 1940's. All
of them were successes outside the pulp field as
well - Zagat working for the government and with
various writing groups; Blassingame as an author of
numerous hardcover and paperback mystery novels;
Burks as a prolific author as well as noted lecturer;
and Page who left the fiction field to make his mark
working on the Atomic Energy Commission and authoring
several Presidential Reports. What ties these men
and many other pulpsters together is that they were
professionals. It is a sad reflection on too much of
today's fiction that that term can be so rarely used
when describing the authors in question.

Pulp fiction never made any great claims to
lofty thoughts or noble deeds. It was written to
entertain, not to uplift or educate. And in that
one goal, it succeeded admirably. The reason that
it succeeded so well was that the men who worked
for the pulps were full time, professional writers.
Men who cared about their craft. Who worked at
writing - not who wrote because some idea struck them
or they thought it might be a nice way to make some
extra money. These men were writing and selling in

a time when competition was keen and jobs were scarce.
Only the best were able to survive in such a market.
The four authors represented in this collection could
teach many of the writers today a few tricks about
writing entertaining fiction. The flow of these stories
presented here is smooth - that is a word that often
applies to pulp fiction that can rarely be used today.
Their worked flowed on the page. Their job was to entertain - and that is exactly what they did.

   So, we present these stories in the spirit that
they were written - to provide a few hours of entertain-
ment. If they succeed in doing that, we will be satisfied. Knowing the quality of work and the standards of
the authors involved, we know that this goal will be
easily reached!

                              Robert Weinberg
                              Editor & Publisher

Scores of bestial patients fell upon Dr. Clayton and his nurse, Mary, in slavering attack, slashing avidly with pointed teeth. . . . For they thirsted to drink rich blood—quickly—before their healthy clansmen threw them among the wolves of a weird, savage country, to escape the fearful contagion of the loups garous. . . .

THE *Standard*, bearing Doctor Jay Clayton, master surgeon, and Mary Curtin, his nurse, was riding down with ice-coated wings through the white smother of the blizzard, toward Central Canada's Wolf Hollow, which had sent a frantic call for help to the world outside.

The pilot had just said:

"It's Satan's hell-hole, Doctor. Two flyers from my field have had forced landings there. They vanished, leaving

Slaves of the Blood-Wolves

By Arthur J. Burks
(Author of "Through Death's Thin Veil," etc.)

*Novelette of
Eerie, Gruesome
Terror*

blood on the snow. Not even their planes were found."

"Shut up!" snapped Clayton. "Oh, what's the use? We might as well face it, Mary. My father went into Wolf Hollow twenty years ago, came back broken, beaten, with horror-shadows in his eyes. He told unspeakable things about that desolate region."

Mary thought: "I must keep my nerve. It's only this mad, blind flying that has upset the pilot and Jay. We're just a doctor and a nurse, going out to save lives. I must keep remembering."

But she couldn't down the growing terror, which was swiftly squeezing at her heart.

But, "It's all nonsense, Jay," she said. "The inhabitants of Wolf Hollow are not so woefully ignorant and superstitious, or they wouldn't have sent out their call for help."

Mary couldn't see Clayton's eyes, but she knew that her terror was somehow reflected in them, so that she did not need to look. Cold that had nothing to do with the blizzard outside, chased itself along Mary's spine. She kept telling herself:

"I must not be afraid. I've got to prove to Jay that I am worthy of his trust. Twenty people, all at the door of death, and there are only my hands to help Jay's hold them back. Twenty people . . . with more, by now, beside them. . . ."

The earth came up with shocking speed. One moment and there was the blizzard, blanketing everything. In the next moment there were dark splotches on the snow. The splotches, down there, made Mary gasp. They reminded her of the pilot's phrase, "blood on the snow." Then, as the plane dived and righted itself, as the pilot got his bearings with skill and speed, the splotches moved and became human beings wearing furry clothing.

The pilot looked back at Clayton and Mary.

"I'm coming down as far from them as I can," he said. "You pile out, if you're determined to stay. I'm getting away before they can lay hands on my wings. But you'd better change your minds, go back with me. . . ."

Clayton looked at Mary. Mary Curtin shook her head. A great surgeon and his favorite nurse could not be turned back by nameless fears, even though both, being human, felt them to the depths of their souls.

The crate landed. The pilot instantly, when she stopped rolling within a few feet, braked down by the snow, snatched open the door, and literally flung them out. The door slammed, scarcely audible in the storm. Doctor and nurse stared to their right, at the running figures, oddly like wolves moving upright, charging. . . .

The plane taxied, got its wheels off, whitely spinning, and vanished into the blizzard overhead. A dozen unsmiling, swart-faced men, reached Clayton and Mary Curtin, whom they didn't seem to see. They were looking up into the blizzard, with a queer hunger in their faces. Mary Curtin saw the hunger, then she was not at all sure that she had. It was like a red shadow which had passed over the snow-flecked faces; like some queer crimson shadow that flashes, bullet-swift, across the surface of new snow.

A man touched Mary Curtin on the arm, speaking. She whirled, almost screaming. He spoke the French of the French-Canadian, understood by both Mary and Jay Clayton.

"If you're the doctor and his nurse, come with us."

The man's eyes were black, brooding, sullen. He was somewhere around fifty years of age. Clayton and Mary followed, the other men trailing behind in grim, somehow purposeful silence. The leader spoke to them, after a few minutes, over his shoulder.

"My oldest son," he said, "died last night. My next may be dead now, but if he's alive when you see him, and you let him die, it will be the worse. . . ."

It wasn't the words, exactly, but the note of weird menace in the man's voice, which caused Mary Curtin to hook her right arm in Clayton's left one, as though she felt a vast need for his support. She thought, as she followed the Canuck, that his furred back was like that of a bear, standing on his hind feet, fighting off invisible attackers.

She wanted to say: "Jay, let's run away from here. I'm afraid."

But she locked her teeth tightly on the words, so that he might never know how greatly she feared—with what weird apprehension she followed on the heels of Theophile Morin, the leader of that strange band of men with eerie, brooding eyes.

Morin stopped at the snow-splashed door of a long, sprawling log cabin, half the length of an average city block.

"In here," he said gruffly, "and you don't come out until. . . ."

Mary heard no more just then, for out of the cabin strange sounds were coming: moaning sounds, sounds of pain, of weakness unto death, of human terror—sounds that people might make as they fight in ghastly fear, to escape the opening lips of the grave.

But in that moment the two newcomers were the master surgeon, and the perfect nurse, with lives to save. Yet even as they crossed the threshold, Mary thought, hating herself for it:

"I'll wish a thousand times that I had turned back, right here, and deliberately left them to die!"

She thought of the pilot, getting away, of the hands of the natives, reaching for his wings, missing, and staring after the vanishing airman with awful hunger in their eyes.

And then, Mary Curtin, from her efficient five feet seven, looked down into the pinched white, frightened faces of her patients, the terror dying for a moment, then leaping up with a fresh, hellish flame.

The first patient she saw was a young man perhaps twenty years of age. There were tiny flecks of fresh blood on his chin.

THEOPHILE MORIN had gone in with them, bidding the others remain outside. Clayton barked at Mary Curtin, and the great surgeon and his nurse were busy. Clayton lost himself in his profession but it was different with Mary Curtin. She lifted her eyes to the windows against which wind had pelted the snow.

The palms of the natives of Wolf Hollow who had remained outside were describing circular movements outside the panes rubbing away the snow laboriously, making clean spaces into which the snow kept ceaselessly beating, then pressing their faces against the glass. Their hot breath became steam against the panes, and the steam formed strange shapes on the windows. . . .

Inside, men and women, on rough pallets, on the bare floor, some of them nude, were quartered together chaotically.

Clayton got busy with his instruments, examined each one with sure, professional speed, removed his stethoscope, stared at Morin. Fear was in his eyes as he foresaw the effect of his diagnosis.

"Pernicious anemia, Morin," he said. "They need blood. They need plenty of blood. . . ."

The effect on Morin was strange, horrible. Murder looked out of his eyes together with another expression Mary could not define. Theophile, as Clayton had done, licked his lips. But the lip-licking of Theophile was different than that of Clayton, with a horrible, *hungry* difference. Mary couldn't define it, but all at once she felt a constriction of the throat which brought a dread picture to her mind: a picture of herself, supine in the snow, her throat bare, and Theophile bending over her, pawing at her, his bearded lips close to the great vein. . . .

Theophile began to cackle weird, horrid laughter.

"Blood? Blood? Sure, they all want blood. Everything wants blood! Listen!"

The whole moaning horror-house seemed to pause to listen. From somewhere outside, now near, now far, seeming to encircle Wolf Hollow, came the ghastly sound of wolves racing in a pack, seeking food, giving tongue. Cold sweat showed on the face of Jay Clayton. For the first time in her experience as a nurse, Mary Curtin was afraid that her knees were going to let her down to the floor, among the emaciated remnants of what must once have been strong men and women.

But her eyes went to the windows, each in turn, to see that the faces there had moved. Only the sides of them were visible, as though, at a signal, the men who had greeted them on landing had turned to listen to the wolves.

"Just wolves," said Jay Clayton. "That's all. What makes them come around here?"

Theophile Morin's chuckle was horrible to listen to as he answered.

"Why shouldn't they? Most of them are the dead, already thirsting for the living, because they needed blood, too, when they died!"

Clayton jumped to stand before Morin. Every patient in the place had heard his words, and their moans were moans of abject terror, their eyes wide, staring, fearful, as their ears heard the howls of the wolf-pack.

"Shut up, you mad fool!" snapped Clayton. "Don't you know better than to say such things where the patients can hear?"

"Fool, am I? And why shouldn't I speak out, so's they'll know? Listen, Doctor Jay Clayton, son of Leslie Clayton, to what I'm telling you! Those wolves need blood because they died needing it, leastwise some of them, and the werewolves that run with the wild pack. How do I know? Because, as our people died we tried to bury them in the snow, be-cause the ground under the snow was frozen too deep to be dug. The wolves dug them out, ate them, got their blood, what was left of it. Those wolves that ate, became the humans they ate. Now, hark ye, we merely throw the dead into the snow. And why not? If we save them the wolves will come for them, wherever they are. Better that they eat the dead than the living. . . ."

Jay Clayton slapped Theophile Morin once on either side of the face. The man's shaggy head rocked and rolled with the blows, and his cheeks became red.

"You'll pay for that," said Morin, "but first you'll save our people."

From outside rose snarls of protest as the men at the windows saw the manhandling of their leader. Mary noted the bared teeth, looking horribly suggestive, when one saw them and listened at the same time to the baying of the wolves.

"Cut out the nonsense," said Clayton, "and get this. These people have pernicious anemia. They must have blood, understand? I've got to perform transfusions on all of them, right away, or some of them will die. . . ."

"If they die, the pack will feast—off a fool doctor and a pretty nurse!" railed Theophile Morin.

Clayton's face showed grim resolve as he shook Morin's shoulders.

"Listen, fool," he said. "If you do as I bid you, and we fail to save most of these people, then you are welcome to throw me to the wolves. . . ."

"And me with him," said Mary Curtin quietly.

"Now who are the fools?" said Theophile, cackling his weird laughter. "It's plain you don't know much about Wolf Hollow. Your dad could have told you . . . but what do you want?"

"Bring in all your healthy men, for blood tests. The blood has to be just right. We can't get anyone in from outside.

Residents of Wolf Hollow must do. They must furnish the blood . . . ."

THE face of Theophile Morin worked strangely, crazily. He was mumbling now, his lips writhing, his eyes almost popping from their sockets.

"What difference does it make? We give blood to these. They die. Our blood goes to the wolves. Why not cast ourselves before the wolves?"

"Do as I bid you, or these will die," Clayton insisted grimly, "and if what you say is true, they will be devoured, creating more werewolves which, in the end, will get you anyhow. . . ."

A look of cunning came into Morin's eyes. He shook a dirty finger in Clayton's face.

"I'll do what you say, Clayton," he said. "But there'll be no nonsense. I know you city men. If you don't save these ones, and don't make sure what finally happens to the blood, you'll be thrown to the wolves, right enough; but not before this nurse has been given to . . . ."

He cackled and turned to the windows, his black eyes roving over the faces that seemed to be frozen there, teeth showing in silent, moveless snarls. It seemed to Mary in that moment that every pair of eyes was fixed on her, probing through her clothing, disrobing her. She heard herself, as though hers had been the voice of a stranger, telling Theophile—

"I will not resist, if you do what Doctor Clayton says, and the doctor fails. I have that much confidence in him—that most of these sick ones will be saved."

"Most?" repeated Theophile. "All, Doctor, nurse; all, do you hear me? *All*, or you know what'll happen to both of you!"

Clayton said:

"Bring, besides those outside, all healthy men and women in Wolf Hollow. Mary, prepare the instruments for the tests."

Mary busied herself with her work. Her face was very white. The voices of the wolves came from outside, now white-black night. In fancy she could see pointed fangs tearing at helpless flesh. In reality she could see bearded faces at all windows, gums skinned back from white teeth in soundless snarls; could feel the probing, savage eyes.

The door opened, letting in a great gust of wind, and a lacy tracery of wind-driven snow spewed across the floor. Three came in, to stand before Mary Curtin and the doctor. There were more faces at the windows now, some of them of women, of girls; and their teeth, too, were showing, while their black eyes were filled with superstitious suspicion.

The tests began. Clayton began to draw some blood from the sturdy arm of a man. . . .

"Hold him! Hold him for me!"

It came in a hoarse croaking, from behind Mary. She whirled, almost dropping cotton and bandage in spite of her usual iron will. One of the patients, a boy of eighteen, was crawling toward them on hands and knees. His tongue was caress-his lips. His eyes were wide, staring, his face filled with hunger, at sight of the blood Clayton was taking from the arm of one of the potential donors. As Mary looked the boy lifted from his knees, so that he shambled oddly on hands and bare toes, over the cold floor. . . .

The last touch of horror came when the baying of the pack, out in the night, rose suddenly to a shrill crescendo, as though the boy's change of locomotion had been a ghastly signal.

Mary forced herself to do what she did next. She went to the boy, lifted him in her arms, his nude, dirty chest against her breast—his body light, bony, with the wasting of his disease—and whispered to him:

"Don't worry, darling, you'll be all right."

The boy's lips quested for her neck. She lowered him, fighting to repress a shudder. She placed him on his pallet again, his face to the wall, so that he could not see the spots of blood. Mary came back to Clayton. Their eyes met.

"The exertion almost finished him. He's too weak to turn and look again. If he isn't the first to be treated, he'll die. . . ."

Her neck seemed to throb and twist where his hot lips had almost touched her.

CHAPTER TWO

The First Transfusion

THERE was a touch of grim horror in what followed. Jay Clayton might well make a mistake, forfeiting the lives of himself and his nurse. Yet he went about his work, shutting out all other considerations, as though he were performing a simple tonsillectomy in his own hospital. Mary Curtin's heart went out to him for his rare courage, though she could not know that even in the midst of the desperate plight shared by both, his heart went out to her for the same reason.

Men were tested, and women, and swifter than it would ever have been considered advisable in the realms beyond Wolf Hollow. But necessity drove Clayton to perform miracles. He found the right people, healthy, robust, untouched by disease.

He performed transfusions on all of the patients, beginning with the youngster who had tried to fasten his sharp white teeth in the neck of Mary Curtin. Even as he worked he wondered how it happened that almost every patient, when first encountered, had flecks of dried blood on lips or chin, as though each had bitten into his or her own tongue in agony. But he examined the tongues, and there were no marks of self-biting. . . .

The patients, when they had returned to their pallets, which Mary had made as comfortable as possible by dint of heavy labor, seemed, every last one, to be somewhat benefited. Mary devoted her time to them.

But Clayton had something else about which to think. It happened right after the first donor, a big husky man, had given copious blood to an emaciated girl. The men and women not slated to donate blood, because of inherent disease or for some other reason, stood outside, beyond those windows against which their noses were pressed, alternately peering in and looking back to make sure that the wolves were not closing in on them. They stared at the husky one, when, refusing to remain in the building, he staggered forth. He had said:

"They have blood now. Soon they will need more. I do not stay."

Outside the door, the people against the windows raised a shrill clamor.

"Get hence! Leave Wolf Hollow! You have need of blood, because blood was taken from you!"

Horrible incident! For when the startled giver of blood would have joined his fellows, they sent him forth with kicks and blows of their fists, shouting: "Go to the wolves! Stay away from us until your need is satisfied!"

"God," muttered Clayton, hoping that Mary Curtin had not heard or noticed. "What superstition! They send the donors out, believing that they will run with the wolves, and that the wolves will get their blood back by devouring the dead!"

So were the donors placed in ghastly jeopardy, not only of the wolves, but of their own kind. The second in line, noting, would have refused blood, but when he drew back, the people outside, seeing, hammered against the windowpanes with their palms, shouting:

"Give, or our people will die! You are

strong to battle for your own. Give, or refuse to give and die!"

"Sparta," thought Clayton, "never thought of such hardship. If they give of their blood, they die by the wolves. If they refuse, they die by the hands of their own. What manner of people are these of Wolf Hollow? Are they all maniacs?"

Perhaps not, but it was a grim warning of what they were capable of doing. They could reason any way to suit their own superstitions. What chance had Clayton and Mary Curtin against such people? And they were obviously pitted against them, just as Leslie Clayton had been, many years before.

When each of the patients had received his first transfusion, and remaining donors had been bidden to return tomorrow at the same hour, the faces disappeared from the windows. Mary Curtin saw them go, one by one, and wondered why they departed, whether it was the nearer howling of the savage wolves, or something less tangible. What devil's brew were the residents of Wolf Hollow cooking up against the outlanders? Their leaving, with backward, malevolent glances, was far more weird than their presence, outside the windows.

A CHILL that was not of the storm filtered into the log cabin. The patients shivered. Mary pulled the men closer together, and the women, in an effort at rough segregation, and for mutual warmth; and wondered how many of them would live through the night. Theophile Morin's last words had been: "If one dies, cast him out, else the wolves will come for him, and get them all."

Then, Theophile, too, had gone, with malevolent backward glances.

Jay Clayton bade Mary Curtin sleep, and she did not believe she would ever sleep again.

But sleep she did—and wakened screaming. It seemed that Clayton, too, had slept.

It was little wonder that Mary Curtin screamed.

But as she screamed it was not entirely for herself that she feared. Doctor Clayton pushed his way toward her, horror on his face because he saw that their patients, like maggots, were swarming over the woman he loved. She saw that several were clinging to Clayton himself, with feeble hands, their feet dangling off the floor, weakly, while their mouths sought for a resting place upon his hands, his arms, his face. . . .

The log cabin hospital had become a madhouse. While the two tired ones slept the patients they had treated had become, in their own minds at least, ravening white wolves, bent on maiming, destroying, crushing the bones of the doctor and the nurse, to get at the marrow and the heart's blood of the two who were doing the most to make them whole.

Mary Curtin, struggling to her feet, realizing that all these horrible white monsters were too ill in mind and body to know, really, what they did, cried out to Clayton:

"Jay, has there been some horrible mistake? Has something been injected into their veins with the transfusions?"

He was almost beside her. His face was convulsed with horror as his eyes stared into hers.

"Whatever it is," he answered, "it was taken into their veins with the milk of their mothers, as soon as they were born. They are ravening wolves because they think they are, and for no other reason. To them the blood of other people, taken into their own bodies, means but one thing: *werewolves!* They think that is what they have become, and they want more blood. In some fashion, they know they cannot get it from one another—and they can't escape through the door and windows to reach healthy people, except ourselves . . . ."

But even in his horror, his terror for the safety of the nurse he loved showed in his staring eyes. But Clayton remembered that his first duty was to those who would destroy them both.

"Careful, Mary, for the love of God!" he cried. "Handle them carefully. It isn't their fault!"

Even as Mary was struggling up, even as Clayton all but reached her, more victims of the dread disease piled upon her, and she went down, with the ghastly feeling of small white teeth, biting into her neck, her now bare breasts, and of her own blood from the wounds they made, gushing warmly forth, following the curve of her chest to drip upon the icy floor.

OVER and over, Mary Curtin heard that voice droning:

"There is no other blood but theirs! We have benefited from those who have given. More will make us whole again. Catch, and drink. . . ."

Anatole Marcelin was the leader of the white, emaciated attackers. Marcelin, the eighteen-year-old, had quietly massed the patients in an attack against the doctor and the nurse. No medical blunder was responsible for this. It was the superstition of a maddened boy who feared the grave, and would do anything to avoid it. The other patients followed where he led. ·

"Blood will make us well again. Have not the old crones told us! But until now there was no blood. Grasp, hold for your lives, and drink. . .!"

Anatole Marcelin, who already had once tried to caress the flesh of Mary Curtin with his lips—though when he had done that he could have known nothing of transfusions—lunged eagerly to bite into the flesh of her bared breast. She felt it tear between his teeth that seemed razor-sharp. She choked back a scream. She

was terribly afraid, and she was remembering something: the talk of their erst-while pilot, about "blood on the snow," and vanished airmen.

"God," she moaned, trying again to stand erect, to reach the hand that Jay Clayton was extending to her, "other men, and women, suffering with this disease, before Wolf Hollow called on the world for aid, must have sensed their terrible need for blood, or their elders told them —and they captured the stranded flyers. . . ."

She couldn't, even to herself, put the rest of the horrid picture into words. Vanished airplanes, destroyed to the last shred by the inhabitants of this place of horror. Bones had vanished . . . and blood on the snow. . . .

Now her hand grasped that of Jay Clayton. She was lifting herself to her feet. Jay was shouting:

"Try to keep them off you. Try to quiet them. Return them to their beds, one at a time, bind them with something . . . ."

The victims of the dread disease, driven back by doctor and nurse, now turned on one another, and that madhouse, became a hellhouse instead, in which white imps of Satan tried to destroy one another to reach the crimson life-tide that flowed so sluggishly and thinly within the veins of most of them.

"Mary, work faster!" cried Clayton. "They'll kill one another if we don't pull them apart, and we dare not use too much force."

Two were down. One was a man, one a woman. They rolled toward each other, flung their arms about each other's necks in what seemed, at first, a passionate embrace. But, then, they snarled, their mouths opened, and they sought to administer such oscular caresses as to chill the hearts of normal folk.

Even as Clayton told Mary to pick up

one, while he lifted the other, several other patients dropped limply, weakly, or crawled, atop the man and woman who fought for each other's lives, their mouths, already red, wide and gaping, with teeth that were crimson. . . .

When Mary, at last, lifted the girl, she knew that she carried a corpse, a corpse that smiled, a horrible, crimson smile.

The others saw, then, and some became sane, according; perhaps, to the standards of Wolf Hollow, for one yelled: "Werewolf! She-werewolf!"

They knew that the girl was dead. They believed that the wolves would get her, that she would become a werewolf. A cold shudder raced along Mary's spine. Her body seemed to turn to ice when, suddenly, from the thin lips of Anatole Marcelin, tugging feebly at his improvised strait-jacket, came a long-drawn, ululating howl—the howl of a wolf!

"Come for your own, grey ones!" he shrieked, breaking off his mad words to howl again.

Mary Curtin had to work or go mad, for the thin howl had scarcely left the lips of Anatole Marcelin than it was answered from outside by a chorus of snarling animal calls.

"Hurry, Mary, for God's sake!" Clayton yelled.

From Anatole Marcelin, as he died, came another ghastly scream—that of a hunting wolf!

They stared down at him, and at two others who had died almost at the same time, as though his wolf-howl had been a sort of signal.

Some urge she could nderstand caused the nurse to turn, stare at the windows, and then . . . .

Her scream of terror was like a ghastly thunderclap. It turned Jay Clayton's blood to ice in his veins. Her eyes, starting from their sockets, stared at the windows. He turned, and looked.

There were many faces at the windows. At first it seemed that the inhabitants of Wolf Hollow had come back to see how their sick ones fared. But the faces were, they both saw, not human. . . . The gaping jaws, white fangs, red tongues, of wolves; their red eyes peering in, seeming to search everywhere among the prone and supine sick ones, as though they sought for the four who were dead.

Mary Curtin, because she could not help herself, kept on screaming. . . .

WOLVES, thought Mary Curtin, were like dogs, and dogs bayed at the moon and the night when death was near. The wolves *knew*, knew with horrid certainty that there were dead ones in the long log cabin.

Moving together for comfort, Mary Curtin and Jay Clayton stared at the windows that were like black, glaring eyes— beyond which were other eyes. Mad, vengeful, lusting eyes; the eyes of the four-footed denizens of Wolf Hollow, who had given the dread place its name.

Mary's breast rose and fell spasmodically. Through the room now there was a continuous screaming. Several of the patients, in low voices, were calling out: "Give them the dead, or they will break through the windows!"

Well indeed must these sick ones have known the habits of their four-footed enemies of the wilds and the snows of the white wilderness.

Mary looked at Clayton.

"What shall we do?"

"I don't know," he replied. "If we open the door, and cast out the dead . . . ."

Both knew they could not do that. One wolf charged the window—after others had already left crimson frothy foam upon the frosted glass—broke through, and died as Jay Clayton smashed out his brains with a chair-leg twisted from a chair with a maniac's strength.

Clayton dropped the chair-leg, called to Mary:

"Quickly, darling. It will divert the others for a little time. Help me to throw him out."

The body of the wolf was warm to their hands, odorous of carrion—of a horrible, human kind, perhaps—as they pushed against him, forcing him back.

It was the wolf's own kind that finally helped them. They knew death when they saw it. They jumped and fastened their fangs in his drooping hind quarters, helped the two terror-driven people to pull and push him from the window. Their howls were signals to their fellows, all about the cabin. Snouted faces disappeared from the windows. Clayton and Mary stared through the broken panes, Clayton again holding the chair leg, now stained with the wolf's blood. Mary noted the blood and shuddered. How much of it had within its gory stream the lifeblood of human beings?

Outside the grey shapes were piling onto the fallen wolf which Clayton had slain. Clayton forced Mary to turn her head, so that she could not see. Pieces of flesh were ripped from the body of the fallen. Slavering jaws worked with horrible, gulping mastication.

Soon the white ribs of the wolf were there, in the snow, and his blood was everywhere, and red tongues were caressing the red-black splotches.

"They'll finish with the wolf in a few seconds, Mary," said Clayton grimly. "Then they'll be back at the window. It's only a matter of time until they'll gain entry. The wolves know that if one window can be broken, all of them can . . . and they are too many for us. There are too many windows to be guarded. . . ."

Mary looked bravely into his eyes, trying to mask the terror in her own. They were doomed. Their eyes told it to each other.

"We could stave them off for a time, by tossing . . . through the window . . . ."

Mary's face was very white as she shook her head.

"I couldn't do it, Jay," she said. "And I'd hate you to the grave if you did it. We're human beings, Jay, as are these people who act as our enemies, because they know no better. The dead have a right to our protection, as much as have the living. . . . No! No!"

"You understand what it means, then?"

"Yes."

Clayton whirled, went to his kit, took out a revolver, gave it to Mary.

"When they come in," he said, "shoot until you have one cartridge left. Count them to make sure. There are now six in the weapon. When you have used up five, shoot the last into your own brain."

She took the weapon leadenly, as though she were moving in strange hypnosis.

"And you?" she said.

"I'll use some surgical instrument," he retorted gravely. "Now, back to the broken window. It will be the first they will try."

He looked out, holding Mary back, so that she could not see. Already the wolves, beating the snow flat about the skeleton of one of their number, questing hungrily for stray morsels, for more splotches on the snow, were lifting grey and black muzzles at intervals, to stare at the window.

ANATOLE MARCELIN, now dead, had brought the wolves with his death-scream. Mary remembered, crept closer to the window. She couldn't help herself. She had to see. Wolves looked up at her, crouching low, as though to spring in any direction, and showed their fangs.

"Jay," whispered Mary. "Jay, am I going mad, or do some of the wolves look like human beings, crouched on all fours?"

Clayton did a strange thing then. He whirled on Mary, whom he loved, who knew that he loved her, and slapped her face. The blows were numbing shocks, setting her back on her heels. But somehow they released her from a kind of paralysis, drove the mad ideas from her head. . . .

"Help! Help!" yelled Clayton. "I wonder why I didn't think of that before," he told Mary. "It may not be of any use, but we should exhaust every possibility. Help! Help!" His voice went cannonading through the storm. The wolves drew back, looked apprehensively to the north, in which direction the inhabitants of Wolf Hollow had gone. One grey beast leaped at Clayton, who had thrust his head partially from the window to give full range to his shout. Sharp fangs almost touched Jay's throat. He drew back swiftly. There were jagged shards of glass clinging in the window-frames. He cut his neck on one, and the blood streamed. The smell of it drove the wolves to fresh madness.

The patients were screaming weakly, in a horrid monotone.

Then, through the curtain of snow to the north, Clayton made out the flashing of torches.

"They're coming, Mary," he said.

The wolves, seeing the torches, hearing the shouts of the denizens of Wolf Hollow, were massing in ragged formation to meet them. Clayton stared, straining his eyes. A score of men were coming, led by the mighty Theophile Morin. Their left hands carried blazing knots. Their right hands held stout cudgels.

The wolves hesitated, as though checking the odds against them, estimating whether they could fight successfully.

Then, giving tongue, they charged.

The people of Wolf Hollow charged to meet them, swinging cudgels and pine

knots. They struck out. A wolf fell. His fellows leaped atop him, rending, tearing. The people of the Hollow attacked the tumbling mass of grey with savage cudgels. The men were shouting, and their voices mingled grimly, suggestively, with the snarling and yowling of the wolves, as though the men and their enemies had been blood relations. . . .

Then the pack concerted all their numbers in an attack on their human enemies. The inhabitants of Wolf Hollow formed a wedge, ringed about by blazing knots and cudgels, and raced for the door of the cabin. There they put their backs against the door, forming a semi-circle.

Theophile Morin came in, stared around, saw the four who were dead, and one of them his son.

"I warned ye!" he said.

He turned, look at the door, through which came the sounds of conflict.

"They'll stay fighting," he continued, "and bringing others to help them fight, out of the forest, until there are too many of them, and they will beat us, unless. . . ."

His eyes went to the dead. If there were any paternal love in his face when he looked at his emaciated, dead son, Mary Curtin could not see it.

"Give us our dead," he muttered thickly. "Give us our dead. We can keep them off now, long enough to drive the stakes in . . . !"

"Stakes?" asked Clayton. "What do you mean by stakes?"

Theophile snarled, his teeth skinning back.

"City folk are ignorant," he snorted. "Stakes to drive through the hearts, of course, so that the dead will stay dead, and not become *loups garous!*"

Neither Mary nor Jay could speak for a moment, listening to this horrible suggestion, in which Theophile and his people so obviously believed, this grim, ghastly interpretation of the stake driven through the heart of the dead, to prevent their becoming—not vampires, as in the common legend—but werewolves.

Theophile called in two men.

Slowly, one by one, they bore out the bodies. Mary and Jay stood, watching, their arms about each other.

The door closed. Thudding sounds came through, the sounds of blows, of blows against stakes—driven with hammers of horror that smashed against the brains of Mary and Jay.

"Jay," whispered Mary at last, "do you know what that means? It means that we, too, before we die, will know the stakes, before the wolves get us! By their reasoning they'll *have* to do it, to keep us from coming back on all fours to avenge ourselves!"

Finally the sounds ceased. The wolves were going away, stalking the flanks of the men who bore the dead, and those who fought off the wolves, until they were ready. In fancy, Mary could see the naked dead being borne swiftly along, toward the forest, and behind them, unless tracked out by their bearers, drops of blood were being left on the snow, falling from ghastly wounds made by the stakes. . . .

CHAPTER THREE

Fresh Blood for the Morrow

WHO, in God's Name, wondered Mary, could believe in this living nightmare? There couldn't, anywhere in the modern world, be people so ignorant and superstitious. And yet, vanished airmen . . . wolves dashing through the snow to peer through the windows, seeking the dead . . . men who looked, in their furs, like wolves themselves, their small brains seething with horrible superstitions.

Mary and Jay looked at each other.

Jay shrugged.

"We've got to keep going," he said dully, "or we shall go mad, and race out into the snow to throw ourselves to the wolves. Work, Mary, work, and work more!"

She nodded. There were still many things to be done for the sick. Hot water to be heated, applications to be made to the wounds the instruments had made, the wounds made by the teeth of their fellows. The log cabin gradually became a hospital again. Outside, through the storm, the yowling of the wolves had died down, and both were resolutely trying to shut from their minds the surety of the reason why. The wolves were feasting, too busy to give tongue.

Would Mary and Jay live to see another dawn? How had Jay's father, twenty years before, escaped this place with his life? Morin had known Leslie Clayton. Morin had been a young man then, with the beliefs of his people firmly gripping him. Since that time they must have grown, become obsessions—and Theophile Morin led his people in Wolf Hollow. What he thought, they thought.

No wonder the white wilderness was a madhouse!

What must it be like to spend a night in one of their cabins, where every eerie cry in the night from outside was interpreted in terms of the *loup garou?*

"Don't think, Mary," said Clayton. "Work!"

Patients to be made more comfortable. Waking patients to be comforted. Blood-flecks to be washed from thin, drawn lips and white chins. Fear to be driven from staring eyes with gentle words of soothing quality. In doing all this, with Clayton beside her, everywhere in the cabin, Mary forgot some of her own terror.

The city was a dream. This nightmare was real. Nothing else was. The wolves were a present, tangible menace; so was

Theophile Morin. Mary wondered what would happen next. . . .

"Go to sleep now, darling; it's all a dream that's ended. We're here, the doctor and I, to make you well, to keep the terrors away. Sleep, and don't be afraid." Thus she soothed those suffering souls.

With her face washed clean, a puny girl, to whom Mary talked, looked like any other girl, with the terror leaving her eyes when she drank courage from those of Mary. Then she questioned:

"I'll have new, fresh blood tomorrow, nurse?"

"Yes," Mary answered, shuddering.

Clayton looked out the window again. "They're coming back," he said quietly. "There is a woman with Theophile, who leads them. . . ."

"The wolves?"

"Not the animal ones, the human ones —the people of Wolf Hollow."

"The wolves are not following," said Clayton, "but the men keep looking back, as though expecting them to charge from the rear at any moment."

"They'll be here in a minute, Mary," he said. "We must be ready for anything. No telling what the madmen will do. Have you still got the revolver?"

"In my pocket," she answered.

"Remember, use it on yourself rather than . . . rather than . . . ."

THEOPHILE came through the door, with the woman. His lips, for the first time, were split in a grin. But it was an evil grin, suggestive of a lunatic's cunning. Its apparent friendliness was a lie, and yet. . . .

"Maybe I been wrong, doctor," he said. "Maybe all these sick ones are too much for you and the nurse. I've brought help. She's a midwife, and she's a good hand with other kinds of sickness. Could she help, as your nurse helps?"

Clayton suspected something, but he temporized. They did need help, and except when there were transfusions to be performed, any intelligent woman could serve him.

"It's simple," he said. "All she has to do is what I tell her."

"You're sure, doctor? Even if you didn't have that nurse here, Clarice could help you just as much?"

"Almost. When it's time for more . . . for more. . . ."

"More blood," finished Theophile. "Tomorrow evenin'. I understand that. But by that time, maybe you could teach her enough to help . . . ?"

Clayton could not see whither the cunning Theophile was leading, but he followed the lead anyhow.

"I think so. After another transfusion all around, Theophile," he said. "I could leave the patients with Clarice, and if she carried out my instructions to the letter, these patients would get well."

Theophile moved a little closer.

"The wolves are many tonight," he said. "They want for more flesh, more blood. But they shan't have any more of the sick ones. They must live, understand? That's why I brought Clarice. If, as you say, she could help as well as this other, then . . . ."

"Then?"

"Then we'll cheat the wolves, or keep them off for a while. They're not needing much more . . . ."

Suddenly, Theophile moved with the speed of light, his great arms went around Mary Curtin. She screamed, tugged the revolver from her clothing as Theophile lifted her shoulder high, stared over at Jay Clayton.

"We'll satisfy the wolves with the one stranger you won't be needing, Doctor," he said, turning, leaping for the door, carrying Mary Curtin as though she had been a bag of feathers. "But don't be fretting, the stake will save her from becoming . . . ."

With a cry of agony Jay Clayton dashed after Thèophile. But the door closed in his face. Through the panels came the screams of Mary Curtin.

Just inside the door was the revolver he had given Mary, useless now to aid her. Her screams were dying away as Theophile raced outward from the cabin, toward the ranging wolves.

Jay Clayton whirled back, staring at Clarice. The woman was laughing wildly, slapping her thighs resoundingly.

"Tricked ye!" she said. "Tricked ye, and ye a city man!"

Jay came to a swift decision. If he left, and the wolves dragged him down, these sick ones would die. If he did not go, there wasn't a hope in the world for Mary Curtin.

And the man won over the doctor, at least partially, for Jay Clayton paused long enough to give terse instructions to the woman, adding:

"I'll be back, if I live, to save these lives, only when your people promise me that the girl and myself go free, unhindered. Tell them that when they come. . . ."

Then he went out through a window, crashing through the bits of furniture he had stuffed in it. Clarice would know enough to plug the hole after he had gone.

He carried the crimsoned chair-leg, tightly gripped in his right hand.

As a guide to him Mary's scream came out of the wind and snow, from somewhere westward, and over beyond it, coming closer, sounded the yowling of the wolves. Clayton ran low against the ground, his eyes straining through the lacy tracery of the blinding snow, seeking the mighty bulk of Theophile, with Mary Curtin in his arms, bearing her as

a peace offering to the scavengers of the white wilderness.

CHAPTER FOUR

The Ring of Fire

MARY, riding high on the shoulder of Theophile Morin, knew that she was doomed. She struck at his shaggy head, ripped at his face with her fingernails. Theophile grabbed her wrists, chuckled.

"I like 'em savage," he said. "But you'd better stop, white face. Or would you prefer Theophile to the wolves?"

His hands began to play over her. She shrieked: "Let it be the wolves!"

He chuckled. "I expected that. City women don't appreciate *men!*"

If his hands and arms had not been needed to guard his body against her clawing fingernails—if Theophile had been able to continue his pawing—Mary would have gone mad. His hands made her think of the paws of a shaggy wolf.

"What are you going to do?" she asked.

"Meet my people. We drive the stake. You are tossed to the wolves. It will satisfy them long enough for us to get back to the cabin, where we can fight them off. They'll go away with the dawn. The sick ones will have more blood before night comes again. . . ."

Mary now was too numb to scream. She twisted, finally, looking back without hope. Clayton would never leave fifteen patients to die, in order to save one woman. She would never ask it of him. And yet when, far behind, she saw a stooping figure coming, running, she could have cried aloud for joy.

But the inhabitants of Wolf Hollow were coming, too, and behind and around them were the wolves.

Then she lost Jay in the smother behind. Perhaps the wolves had pulled him down —those skulking brutes she had passed on the shoulder of Theophile Morin. Her heart sank. The end was approaching, horrible, inexorable.

Abruptly, a figure catapulted from the woods to her left a little behind Theophile, unseen to him. Jay's teeth were bared, as though he had been himself a leaping wolf. His cudgel crashed home. Theophile Morin fell in the snow. He was blinded, half unconscious, when Jay Clayton caught Mary in his arms, ran straight into the woods with her, to be out of sight before Theophile could gather his scattered senses.

"Our patients, Jay," said Mary.

"Can die for all of me," he answered. "You're more to me than the lives of a thousand patients. . . ."

She should have rebuked him, but all she could say was, "Jay! Jay!"

Deeper, deeper into the woods they went. She doubted that Theophile's people had seen what had happened.

Only the wolves would find their tracks in the snow. Jay ran with her until his panting breath rasped his lungs. Then he set her down, and they ran on.

"Watch for dead trees, Mary," he gasped. "I've got an idea!"

Finally they crashed into a small deadfall. Behind them the wolves were giving tongue.

"Quickly, Mary," said Jay Clayton. "Break off the dead wood. Form a circle about us. . . ."

They worked at top speed, building what looked like a fort.

Even then the grey shapes—almost black—of scattering wolves, could be seen against the wilderness. They worked until, even in the cold, perspiration bathed their bodies.

"Here, Mary, the only matches we have. Guard them as though they were jewels."

She took them, thrust them in her breast, against the warm flesh.

Now the wolves were closer. They could see their lolling tongues. Clayton took his stance, with the cudgel.

"Fire the wood," he said, "if they get past me. Now, crouch down against the bole of this fallen tree, understand? I'll stand over you. The wood must somehow save us until dawn, when Theophile says they will go away.

And then, the first grey wolf charged, and Jay Clayton forgot that he was the master surgeon, forgot everything, and became a cave-man—a killer. . . .

He met the wolf in mid-charge, brought the cudgel down with all his power behind it. More potent, this cudgel, he told himself, than would have been the revolver he had forgotten to scoop off the floor of the cabin, in his crazed anxiety to reach Mary.

The wolf was driven back by the savage blow—not killed but knocked to earth. And a fallen wolf, among this hunger-crazed pack was doomed as though already dead. The grey mass of them were all over the fallen one in an instant, tearing, rending. Mary covered her face with her hands.

Clayton was everywhere around the inside of the circle of wood. There was another reason why he didn't fire it. The inhabitants of Wolf Hollow would see the flames, and come, drive off the wolves, and give Mary to them.

IT WAS cudgel against fang. Clayton struck again and again, with the power of a madman in his blows. He was estimating time. By now the people would have found Theophile, if the wolves hadn't got him. They would be going back to the cabin, wondering, afraid of what manner of woman Mary was, that she had escaped even the powerful Morin. Then, back there, Clarice would tell them, and they would be sure that the wolves, by this time, had got both Mary and Jay.

He heard a sound.

The teeth of Mary Curtin chattering, not with fear, but with cold.

A wolf reached Jay, ripped at his shoulder. Its fangs bit deeply. Blood flowed, and the others, smelling it, went mad. They charged from all sides.

"No use, Mary," said Clayton, striking out, battering away. "Fire the wood!"

"My fingers are so cold I can't bend them!"

"Fire the wood!"

The urgency in his voice seemed to do it, for a flame licked into the dead branches, flared high, straight into the grey face of a monster leaping the frail barrier. The beast sank back. The flames went higher.

The barrier was ablaze. Jay gathered up handfuls of snow to throw upon it, so that it should not burn too fast. The wolves slunk back, fearing the fire, watching as the flames burned low. Then, bellies close to the ground, they closed in. Clayton, once, dared to charge in among them with flailing cudgel, and almost lost his life.

Back inside, panting, spent, he waited. It was a silent battle between the wolves and the red flames. . . .

Finally one of the wolves rose, howled, trotted off through the woods, vanished— and Jay Clayton knew that dawn was creeping through the white wilderness. Soon all the other grey creatures went off.

At the same time, faint and far away, from out of Wolf Hollow, came shouting voices.

"Quickly!" said Jay. "Cover the charred wood. The place must look as though there had been no fire. If we can make them believe that we spent the night among the wolves, and were not slain. . . ."

She got the idea. They covered the remnants of the fire with snow.

"Won't do," said Jay. "They're woodsmen; they'll smell the smoke in the air."

"Let them find us then," said Mary, "walking toward them, unharmed, from the area where the wolves howled through the night."

And so Theophile and his men found them walking, unafraid, through the woods. They stared, and would not believe, when Jay Clayton said:

"The wolves did not bother us, Theophile. See, we are whole and alive! Clarice told you? If we are not promised immunity from you, and from the wolves, I will never go back to the sick, understand? They will die, and. . . ."

"The promise is given," said Theophile heavily, "for what use is there to do otherwise than promise people who are stronger than the grey brothers?"

"Do the people of Wolf Hollow keep their promises?"

Theophile straightened his shoulders with pride.

"No native of Wolf Hollow has ever broken a promise!"

Mary and Jay, in the midst of the superstitious ones, exchanged glances. The inhabitants of Wolf Hollow fed their own to the wolves, murdered strangers, believed in *loup garous,* in driving stakes through the bodies of the dead, in all the black magic known to ignorant mankind —but they were proud that they never broke their promises!

So the doctor and the nurse returned to their patients, and presently the sky was freed of the blizzard and beyond the dread region of Wolf Hollow, among normal people, the press of two countries still waited, little guessing what their story would be when they told it—with hushed voices, as though they spoke of nightmares that had been real. . . .

THE END

In the January Issue—

Feature-Length Mystery Novel

DAUGHTER OF THE PLAGUE
By Hugh B. Cave

The story of John Paine's terrifying ordeal when he was lured
by the cunning of a jealous woman into the devil's workshop!

Satan Sends a Woman

By WYATT BLASSINGAME

(Author of "Models for Madness," etc.)

Ed Roland, the man who had never known fear, shrieked and grovelled in stark terror when he fell into the snare of that eerie woman who was more beautiful than life—more horrible than death. . . .

"THERE are different kinds of courage," Ed Roland said. "A mad bull elephant will charge almost anything on earth, and will run from a mouse. Smiling, a woman can face death through child-birth, and will

scream at a tiny sound in the dark. There is nothing on God's earth that is totally without fear."

His voice had an odd, strained sound, but at the same time it rang as though those sentences had been repeating themselves over and over in his brain for years. I stopped the julep halfway to my lips and looked at him. Once more the feeling, half fear, half amazement, that I always experienced when I saw him, came over me.

He was sitting on the top step of the porch. His feet were drawn up close to his haunches, his arms were akimbo; he looked like a spider, with his long arms and legs reaching out from a small, round body. There was something about his face, too, which had always reminded me of a spider, hideous, with large, round eyes that are impossible to describe. Looking at him I always got the impression that once he had been a big man, perfectly built, perhaps handsome. But God knows he was ugly enough when I knew him.

Perhaps it was the way he looked, as much as the thing he said, that made me stop the julep, elbow half bent. The moonlight, sliding past the eaves of the house, barely touched him. The small, flower-covered yard was liquid silver in its light, and dark pines loomed up tall and slender, to lean their wide-flung arms on the shoulders of heaven. Beyond them the gulf of Mexico was as placid as a blue mirror with a glittering silver frame of sand.

"What do you mean, there are different kinds of courage, Ed?" I asked. "You sound as though there were a story behind it."

"You might call it a story; I've never known." He sat there for a long time looking like some huge spider backed against the porch. I took a pull on the

julep, burying my nose deep in the mint. "I'll tell you," he said. "Maybe you'll call it a story. All I know is—it happened." After a moment he began to talk.

IT was a man called Paul Jenkins who who first said that about "kinds of courage." I had never seen him when I got the note asking me to come to his hotel room in Mobile. The note sounded interesting, and I went.

"I know you've got courage," Jenkins told me after we had talked a few minutes. "But there are different kinds of courage. I know you are not afraid of bullets and knives, but how about other things? How about swamps where two or three inches of water covers everything, and below the water the mud is without bottom? How about snakes, thousands of them? And how about—?" He paused, his mouth open and a queer, frightened look in his eyes.

I said, "All right, how about it?" I had never been afraid of anything and didn't think I could be. It may sound funny to hear me say that, when you see the way I appear now. But at that time I didn't look like this. I was handsome enough then to get into trouble with women wherever I went, and that was the main reason I was listening to this man's proposition. I was involved with a married woman in Mobile, and was ready to get out. I hadn't met her husband and didn't want to, because she was rather well placed in the city and a scandal would have hurt. So I said, "All right, what do you think I might be afraid of?"

Jenkins licked his lips. "There's probably nothing worse in Death's Swamp than the bogs and snakes. But nobody goes far in there—and comes out. Persons around the edges are superstitious. Perhaps the whole story is superstition, but anyway I'm willing to pay you a thousand dollars to find out."

"For a thousand dollars I'll bring you back a ghost," I said. "Spill it."

Well, maybe you know already the legend of which Jenkins spoke. A ship, carrying a fortune in pearls, was supposed to have been wrecked on the far side of the swamp, about five years ago. There was no way to reach the place except through the swamp, because a boat coming in from the gulf would be caught and wrecked, as this one had been. Nobody was certain, however, for every person on the wrecked ship had vanished. Legend said that a few had gone to investigate, but none ever came back.

"A sailor who claimed to have seen the hulk of the ship from the gulf, gave me the location," Jenkins confided. "I'll give you a thousand to investigate. If the ship's really there, and you find the pearls, we'll split. If the ship's not there, the thousand's yours."

"What if it's there?" I asked. "How do you know I won't take the pearls and skip? We never saw one another until an hour ago. What's your guarantee?"

He was a big man with a square, hard mouth, and when he grinned there was something savage about it. "How do I think I know you might be willing to try this?" he asked. "I've investigated you for weeks, and I'll gamble on your word to play fair."

"Okay," I said. "Now where is this place?"

TWO days later, without saying anything to Ann Bentley, I left Mobile, the thousand dollars already in my pocket.

I had forgot what Jenkins had said about different kinds of courage, until twilight started settling heavily around me. I had been in the swamp since sunrise and knew I should be getting close to the gulf shore. Above the trees light was still in the sky, but the swamp was dark with a heavy, almost tangible gloom. It wasn't black, but there was a sort of murky greyness that pushed vision back against my eyes. Long, coiling vines came suddenly to strike against my face, and I knew that snakes would give no more warning than the vines. I could hear them in the water, only a few inches from me sometimes, as I poled the flat bottomed boat, and now and then I caught the glimmer of white that meant a cottonmouth moccasin had bared its fangs. The pole sank into the bottomless stuff below the water with each stroke, and my wrists and shoulders ached from tearing it out.

It was then that those words about kinds of courage came back to me and I began to understand what Jenkins had meant. I wasn't afraid, yet there was a feeling inside me that had never been there before: a kernel of dread that might burst open at any moment and loose its tendrils around my heart. I knew that it wasn't the snakes or the quicksand that put that feeling inside me. Dangers of that kind had been meat and drink to me for years. It was something else, something in the gloom and in the very feeling of the place.

"Maybe I ought to tell myself a ghost story," I joked to myself, grinning. I forgot the feeling for awhile, and began to wonder what Ann Bentley would do when she learned I had left Mobile. Probably storm about the house for a half hour or so, then find herself another lover. "Her husband will get back in time to look after the next one," I thought, and laughed.

It was the amazing loudness of the laughter that shocked me, stiffened every muscle in my body and made my hands jerk tightly around the boat pole. "What the hell?" I said aloud. "There's—" I stopped, mouth open, listening to the tremendous boom of my words.

All at once there was an indescribable coldness along my spine. I knew I hadn't laughed or spoken any louder than usual. It was the absolute, utter stillness of the swamp which had magnified the sounds!

If you have ever been very deep in a cave without lights, you know how the darkness can become so thick that it is like a black, living thing against your face; you *feel* as well as see it. That's the way the silence of the swamp had become; a terrific, furious soundlessness that made my eardrums ache almost to bursting as they strained for some noise. But there was nothing—except that terrible silence that was louder than thunder.

You have no idea how many sounds there are in the air until suddenly they are all gone. You don't hear the crickets, or the frogs, the whisper of wind in the trees, the almost noiseless, multitudinous noises of the swamp that mingle into one low, unnoticed murmur. Then when they are all gone, the silence becomes so sudden that you can almost *hear* it. . . .

I WAS leaning forward on the boat seat, the pole held across my body with both hands, my eyes straining into the grey-black murk of the swamp. I wasn't breathing at that moment and I don't think my heart was beating, or I should have heard its heavy pounding thud. Then I saw the eyes . . . !

They were more than fifty feet away, and yet the glare of them was so intense I had the impression they were almost on me, that they were the eyes of some monstrous animal crouched only a yard off, ready to spring. I tried to cry out, but the words stuck in my throat, hurting. Perhaps it was the pain that brought full consciousness back to me and shook off the terror.

I put the boat pole across the gunwale, very softly, still leaning forward and watching the motionless eyes. With my right hand I found the rifle between my feet, lifted it. I was beginning to smile, crookedly, half ashamed of the terror which I had felt. After all, I thought, they are only the eyes of an animal. At this range I can't miss, even if it comes charging. I snapped off the safety catch, brought the gun to my shoulder.

But I didn't shoot. I can't tell you why. Perhaps the eyes kept me from it, for when I began to study them carefully they didn't seem to belong to any creature I had ever seen. A panther's eyes, reflected in the dark, are terrible, but there is no word for those which blazed at me. They were a furious, hellish red, perfectly round, large and unblinking. They were like two red holes scooped in the darkness; like two red hot coals that had burned everything away from them and were floating in nothingness. In them was an expression of inconceivable lust and hunger.

The rifle at my shoulder, I sat motionless, staring, unconscious now even of the silence that stormed against my ears.

Then, with the suddenness of light, the eyes were gone. For a moment that seemed so long I thought my lungs would burst, because I didn't breathe during it, the silence held. And when the eerie sound came I reeled back in the boat as from a blow, hands shaking, almost dropping the rifle. It was the soft and hideously beautiful laughter of a woman!

There wasn't any mirth in that laughter. Instead there was the same hungry lust that had been in the eyes, a lust that froze the marrow inside my spine.

Life began to return to the swamp then. Far off a frog croaked and the sound was warm and sweet to my ears. Another answered him, and then a cricket set up its lazy humming. I almost cried out in joy without understanding why.

With the blood flowing through my

veins again, my brain began to work. I laughed harshly, cursed myself for a damn fool. It was just a night bird that made the noise, I thought. The eyes—those of some damned animal. Why I didn't shoot it, I don't know. I could have carried it back to Jenkins and told him that it was his ghost. I lit the gasoline lantern in the bottom of the boat, looked at my compass and began to push ahead again. In another mile or two I should reach the coast. . . .

But somehow I couldn't forget those eyes, and all at once the full significance of their ghastly glare struck me. "Good God!" I said aloud. "Even the eyes of a cat have to reflect some tiny bit of light before they'll glow. There wasn't any light back there—no light at all!"

My brain quit working then, frozen on that thought: they couldn't have been the eyes of a panther or any natural animal at all! Then, what kind of *thing* was it?

I CURSED myself for a damn fool, took a long drink from one of the bottles I had brought with me. The liquor burned the dryness from my throat and lay like a warm pool in my stomach, radiating golden lines of heat. "Hell, I'm getting jittery as an old woman," I said, stuck the pole deep in the mud and sent the boat shooting forward. "I take this job because I claim to be afraid of nothing, and the first time I see an animal's eyes in the dark I get chilblains." I began to think of Ann Bentley again and the way she would act when she found that I had left Mobile.

But somehow I couldn't keep my mind on her. The picture of those eyes would come before me time and again, round and hellishly red, unblinking, with that wild, hungry lust burning in them.

I thought, too, of that eerie laugh in which had sounded the sadistic, terrible joy of hell. Like the daughter of Satan,

I thought, then tried to laugh at my own imagination.

Jenkins had been right about "kinds of courage." There was no natural man or beast that, given a rifle and cartridges, I feared. Yet I couldn't forget the look on Jenkins' face when he had spoken of this swamp and the thing that kept men from coming out of it alive.

I came to the end of the swamp almost suddenly. The boat bumped against a few grass hillocks, and then there was no more water. The trees ended, and beyond a slight rise I could hear the unending murmur of the gulf. Taking my knapsack and bedroll, lantern and rifle, I left the boat and walked down to the wide, sandy beach. There was no moon, and when the waves broke they made little glimmering white threads that vanished sharply.

Using the lantern I found driftwood and built a fire where the beach rose into a low bank covered with sea-grape plants. I scrambled eggs, fried bacon and flapjacks, hunger pushing out all thought of the fear that had touched me. But after I had eaten, the feeling came back. Once more I found myself thinking of those eyes and the laugh and the furious, unexplainable silence which had gripped the swamp.

No matter how I tried, I couldn't shrug the feeling off. "Hell," I thought to myself, "there's no need of sitting here all night acting like a baby. I'll get some sleep, and in the morning I'll find whether or not there's any wreck hereabouts."

I began to spread out my bedroll. In the firelight I could see that my hands were shaking. I had never been afraid before, and I had been in some tough spots; so I couldn't understand the feeling which was in me now, the weird, cold shadow of something as ineluctable as death—and more gruesome. All the veins in my body were getting stiff, taut, the muscles contracting upon themselves as though preparing for some hurricane of terror about to strike.

I had spread the bedroll beside the fire and was sitting down to take off my shoes when the first of it broke, with a low, growing sound that came above the unending mutter of the gulf. Someone was running down the beach, madly, blindly, falling, staggering erect, coming on again.

I twisted from the bedroll, caught up the rifle, and with two steps I was beyond the light of the fire, crouched in the darkness.

The thing ran madly. I could hear it fall, claw at the sand until it was on its feet again, then come on. I could hear its breathing, labored agony-torn. Finally it plunged into the circle of light, and stopped.

I had the rifle under my armpit, and when I saw the creature I almost fired as I staggered up, reeling backward, my brain screaming at me that it couldn't be human. Then, the firelight full on its face, I knew that it was only a man, hideous and horribly deformed. I stepped forward, holding the rifle ready.

IN THE second or two before I entered the range of the firelight, I saw him clearly. His head was too big for his body and his hair fell in wild, tangled masses to his great shoulders. A scar slanted downward across his forehead, closing one eye and twisting the right corner of his mouth into a hideous grimace. One leg, shorter than the other, was curiously bent, which explained why he had fallen so often.

The man saw me as I stepped into the firelight. His mouth jerked open in one wild, horrific scream, as thin and fierce as the breaking of a violin string. He lunged through the fire, scattering the burning wood, flinging red sparks high into the air, coming straight toward me. "Stop!" I yelled. "Stop or I'll shoot!"

He screamed again, lunged the last step and hit the muzzle of my rifle with his chest. I don't know why I didn't shoot. Perhaps it was the wild, terrible look in his eyes; perhaps it was because he so obviously didn't mean to harm me. Instead he stood, pushing his chest hard against the rifle muzzle, the scream still thin and terrible in his throat.

I went backward a step, keeping the butt of the rifle tucked under my armpit, my finger curled around the trigger. The slow, creeping terror that I couldn't understand began to crawl through my veins again. There was fear in this man's ugly face, and yet he did not sense the fact that I had almost killed him. If he wasn't afraid of death, then what in God's name. . . ?

"Damn it," I said huskily. "What's wrong with you? Who are you?"

He lunged at me again, caught the rifle with his left hand and pushed the muzzle against his chest. "Kill me!" he screamed. "Kill me! Kill me! For God's sake, kill me quick before she comes!"

Terror and unbelief must have drugged me then, for my only emotion was a dull stupor through which I gazed at the man, my mouth hanging open, my eyes wide. I was accustomed to men unafraid of death. I had seen men fight for life and die grinning. But never before had I seen a man pleading for death, with wild, unspeakable dread blazing in his face. I didn't speak; I couldn't ask him any questions; I just stood looking at him, dazed, stupefied.

"Kill me!" He screamed again, jerking the rifle until I thought the muzzle must crack his ribs. "In the name of God, kill me before she comes!"

"Before *she* comes?" "What the hell do you mean?"

His voice plunged down to a whisper

and his twisted face became a sickly yellow, as though he knew that already he had made too much noise, and it was too late. "She's already done in your boat. I tried to get away in it, but she'd wrecked it. She'll be here in a moment. Please!" His voice went high and shrill again. "Kill me, *now!*" He tried to paw for the trigger, but I jerked away.

"Damn you," I said. "What are you talking about? Who is 'she'?"

"*Desis!*" He hissed the name. "The daughter of hell. I don't know who she is. But she's killed them all. Eaten them! And she'll get me if you don't kill me. Please!"

It was evident this man was mad. I'd seen crazy men before, but somehow I couldn't accept this explanation. The words I used weren't what I should have spoken to calm a man gone insane. "Desis," I snorted. "What the hell are you talking about? That's a type of water spider, poisonous I believe, but I'm not certain."

The man's face went more yellow than ever. The eye across which the scar ran turned into a black hole of horror while the other blazed at me. The crooked mouth jerked so that saliva drooled down across his chin. "I don't know," he sighed. "Maybe she's a spider. Maybe she ain't, but she's hell's—" His whisper stopped sharply, and a silence that was almost titanic smashed against my ears.

It wasn't more than a second that we stood there. Time seemed to have died, while the surf rolled on, slushing over the beach.

Abruptly the man lunged at me and his scream was like thunder torn into one thin, agonizing sheet. "*Kill me! Oh God! Kill me now!*" His left hand pulled the rifle barrel to his chest, his right hand fought for the trigger.

I tore the gun away from him, and the mot' a hurled him sideways, out of the circle of light from the fire. I heard the frantic crunch of his feet on the sand, heard one explosive, whimpering curse. Gradually the silence that was like an utter and absolute darkness shut down on me, soaking up the sound of his running. Then he was gone into the night. I stood almost at the edge of the firelight, rigid, mouth open, unbreathing, eyes wide and peering across the scattered fire into the darkness.

All at once, utterly without sound, she was there!

THE scattered fire made only a pale, thin radiance which touched on the darkness and vanished. She stood at the very edge of the light, her eyes downcast so that I could see only the pale shadow of her lids. Her face was more beautiful than a human being's should be —softly oval with the wide, shadowed eyes that I couldn't see because of the long lashes, a skin that was almost golden and glowing with health, a wide, sensuous mouth. Her hair fell to her waist in a heavy silver cascade that seemed to stir gently though there was no wind. She wore a short skirt made of one piece of cloth tucked about her waist.

The first shock of seeing her was like a blow in the chest knocking the air from me, stopping my heart for a moment. Even in that first instant I began to feel the desire for her tingling through my body, making my blood go hot and jerky in my veins. But I knew also that something was wrong, horribly wrong, though I didn't know what it was. . . .

"Hello," I said finally, inanely. "Where did you come from?"

"I've been here a long time," she said without raising her eyes to look at me. Watching her, that sense of dread came cold and creepy through me, but the sheer power of her beauty drowned out reason.

Abruptly she said, "Won't you put some more wood on the fire? I'm cold."

"Surely." I gathered the sticks the crazy man had scattered, piled them together and put on more wood. The flames began to crackle, the red and gold light of the fire grew brighter. "How's that?" I asked and stood up.

She nodded gratefully, knelt, stretched her hands out to the blaze. The movement stirred the thick, silver hair that was like a mantle about her, and I saw for the first time that she wore no clothes above the waist. Her breasts were high and round, delicately shaped and small.

There was no understanding the passion that burst in me then, shook me like a leaf and stopped the breath in my throat. It was a flame crashing down on me, enveloping my whole body. And with it came, stronger than ever, that uncanny sense of terror.

If she felt shy because of her lack of clothes, she made no move to indicate it. She just knelt there, hands out to the fire that sent flickering shadows across her breasts, eyes downcast.

I became aware of the curious quality of her hair. Its thick, silver sheen seemed to dance in the firelight, as though every strand of it were alive and separate from the others, moving with the gentle undulations of a spider web rocking in the wind. There was something curious, something gruesomely attractive about that hair. I wanted to reach out and touch it, see if each strand were as thin and soft as the spider web it resembled. But when I thought of touching it, a cold shudder shook me.

"It's very good to have a fire," she said, and smiled. Her lips were large and blood-red, but they didn't part with the smile, and I couldn't see her teeth. She had never raised her eyes so that I could look into them. I began to wonder what color they were and why she avoided my gaze.

"I thought this beach was totally deserted," I said, "but it's almost as crowded as Fifth Avenue at Forty-Second Street. "First some idiot comes whooping along here, and now a very beautiful lady."

"Do you think I'm beautiful?" There was something alluring, inviting about her tone, but still she didn't look at me. She didn't have to, for there was no doubting what she meant. With three steps I reached her side of the fire, and during each of those steps horror and passion warred inside me.

"I've never seen anyone so lovely," I murmured, kneeling beside her. My heart was like a rock against my ribs and my mouth was open, fighting for air. My hands trembled as I rested them on my thighs, fighting to keep from throwing my arms around her, crushing her hard against me, my fingers tight against the warm flesh of her shoulders, my mouth hungry against hers. Yet all the while that cold, inexplicable fear writhed inside me.

She turned slightly, her curious hair twisting in the firelight, showing the high mounds of her breasts. One hand came forward slowly, touched on mine, then closed around my fingers. "I've been on this beach a long time," she whispered. "There's been no one here except that— that hideous crazy man. I'm so glad that you've come."

I swayed toward her, my left hand sliding along the warm skin of her forearm. She still had her eyes downcast. Perhaps that was what stopped me; perhaps it was the way her hair had moved, seeming to reach out hungrily for me like a spider web ready to tangle itself about an insect. Anyway I paused, trying to breathe against the fear and passion that stormed inside me.

"Look," I said huskily, "look at me. Raise your eyes. I want to see them."

"Why see my eyes?" Her other hand came out to touch me, and the movement bared both breasts. "You don't want to see my eyes."

She pulled me toward her, and as I responded she lay backward on the sand.

After that, it happened in one tremendous bursting flare of horror when I had lunged toward her. Then, my mouth almost against hers, my head blocking the light from her face, I saw her eyes . . .

They were the round, hellishly red and terrible eyes of the swamp!

Blind with terror I hurled myself away from her. And at that instant my fingers brushed lightly on her hair.

The tiny threads jumped like living things, wrapped themselves around my fingers and half jerked me backward. They had the sleek, tenuous feeling of spider webs and were strong as steel wire. I sent a scream slashing into the stillness, and hurled myself forward in one terrific effort. The clinging hair tore skin from my fingers but pulled loose, and I went hurtling through the darkness, blind with terror, falling, clawing erect, and plunging up the bank and through the sea-grapes. There was only one flaming idea in my brain then: to get away!

Almost suddenly I hit the edge of the swamp, plunged knee deep into muck and water before I could stop. I heard the hissing of a snake, the slither of a body across slime. My feet began to bog deeper. Twisting, I managed to fling myself flat, catch tufts of grass and pull myself from the swamp. Then I began to look about for the boat. I knew I had left it within twenty yards of this place —and I raced up and down the edge of the swamp, sobbing and cursing the darkness.

Reason came back to me slowly. The boat simply wasn't here, although this was the place I had left it. Then I remembered the words of the man who had wanted to die: "She's already destroyed your boat. I tried to get away in it, but she'd ruined it."

I stood dead still, hands clenched at my sides, mouth open, unbreathing. I was trapped with this woman and the man who wanted to die rather than face her!

CHAPTER THREE

Headless Death

IT WAS five minutes later that I regained control of my muscles and brain. By that time I was half a mile away from the place I had camped, the fire hidden by a curve in the beach. I had run until I felt exhausted, and crouched now on hands and knees almost at the water's edge. As my breathing grew more normal my brain began to function again, to battle at the terror which had gripped it. I tried to find some explanation for the things that had happened.

"The man was crazy," I told myself. "I could see that in his eyes. The woman evidently got trapped when some boat sank nearby, or maybe I'm on the wrong beach and she lives around here somewhere." But I thought of her eyes and shuddered.

I tried to convince myself that it was the firelight which had made them so red and hideous. "And her hair—anybody's hair might have got tangled around my fingers, at a time like that. There was nothing strange about her hair." But even then I knew I was lying. No woman had hair as finespun as a spider web and strong as steel. The way it tangled around my fingers was like a web around a fly, like a spider. . . ."

I tried to stop thinking then, but I couldn't. "She looked like a spider," I said half aloud. "There was something about her whole being, her long, slender legs and arms, her small body . . ."

I stood erect, trying to laugh at that, and the sound hurt my throat. "Imagine thinking that *she* looked like a spider." I said. "Why great damn! That was the prettiest woman I ever looked at. I was a fool for jumping up and running, just because her eyes burned redly in the firelight. She'll probably never give me another chance after that fool act, but tomorrow I'll find her and try."

I made no attempt to explain to myself why I didn't want to find her again that night. I knew, though I wouldn't admit it, that I never wanted to see her again—and I knew, too, that I *would* see her, that I could not escape, because she was as unavoidable as death. She *was* death. . . .

"Hell," I said, and laughed again, huskily. "I'm the man who told Jenkins I was afraid of nothing. Now I've let an idiot and a damn good-looking woman frighten me almost out of my wits. I began to walk along the beach, away from the place I had left her.

Some two hundred yards farther, the shore line began to rise into a cliff, and near its base I found a cave. There's not much tide along that part of the gulf, and as well as I could tell the whole cave was above the high water mark. Taking matches from a moisture-tight pack, I began to search the place.

It was fairly long and about ten yards wide with a smooth, sandy floor. Some thirty feet in, the cave bent sharply to the right. "If I build a fire near the back," I thought, "no one outside can see it." Then I cursed myself for a coward, but it was near the back that I built the fire.

THE warmth and the light flickering over the sand gave me courage. I told myself that it was a damn good thing none of my old friends had seen me during the last two hours, or they would never speak to me again: Bill Race and John Burdett who had fought in Chinese and South American revolutions with me, Ed Fuller who had gone with me into a part of Africa where no other white men had ever been; those fellows wouldn't have believed that fear could make a screaming coward of me, as it had done.

With courage running warm in my veins again, I stood up and began to look around me. The floor of the cave was as flat as a table, the sand white and fine. My fire was built against the right wall, the light flickering high up, but not touching the ceiling. Around me, on every side, the dark shadows crouched like some huge animal ready to spring.

I stopped, picked up a handful of the fine sand and let it slide through my fingers. I took a stick, one end of which was burning well, and began to examine the cave more closely.

It's strange how in pitch darkness things brought into a small light seem larger and more vivid than normally, while the light itself appears tiny and lost in the enveloping blackness. The sand seemed abnormally bright under the torch, the little flecks of coral in the cave walls glittered like rubies. But I had the impression that the darkness had swallowed me, that I was lost in the bowels of eternal night and would never find my way back to the fire. I laughed at the sensation, and managed to throw it off. I was still laughing when my right foot struck something that made a dull, crunching sound, and looking down I saw the skeleton.

I felt as though a fist had struck me hard in the pit of my stomach. I reeled backward, the torchlight dancing crazily along the wall. Half the blaze went out, a plume of smoke drifted upward and the darkness rushed in closer to me. Then I checked myself, said, "Damn!" and held the stick carefully until the blaze was bright again. After all, I had seen plenty of skeletons. That wasn't the sort of thing to frighten me.

Holding the stick so that the light fell clearly over the bones, I knelt and examined them. In the cave where no light touched them they had never bleached, but were a moldy grey. All the bones were in perfect order as though the man had died here.

Then I noticed that the head was gone! "Well I'll be damned," I said. "I wonder what carried that off." I leaned over to examine the spine more closely. There were small, chiseled places around it, so that it came to a point like a sharpened pencil. I put out my right hand and touched them.

All at once, as though the touch had shown me beyond doubt, I knew! I didn't move because I couldn't even breathe, and my heart slammed once against my ribs and stopped. *For the marks around that spinal column had been made by human teeth!*

Somehow I shook myself out of the terror which had frozen me, stood up. After all, I had no way of knowing how those marks were made. There were thousands of crabs along the beach. Perhaps they had done it. I swung the light, paused, and stepped forward. There, not three yards from the skeleton, was the skull, its eyeless sockets peering up into the red glow of the torch.

And just beyond the skull was another body, the head missing!

I found three skeletons, all with the heads gone and those peculiar marks around the tops of the spinal cords. Then I went back to the fire, put on more sticks and sat huddled close beside it. I tried to keep my mind fastened on the blaze and the warmth of it against my face and hands. Hell, I was accustomed

to skeletons. I'd seen men die in a dozen countries.

Suddenly I was thinking of the woman, of her eyes blazing at me as my mouth came close to hers. There had been the living fires of hell in those eyes. And I remembered the mad man saying, "She's killed them all! Eaten them!" I thought of the wild sound of his voice pleading for death, and the sobbing curse with which he had plunged into the darkness before the girl's approach.

He had said her name was Desis. That was a type of water spider—and the female spider kills the male, after mating, by biting off his head!

"Good God!" I whispered, staring into the darkness where the headless skeletons lay.

I LUNGED to my feet. I'd spend the night on the beach under the stars, but not here in this cavern of the dead. Not here where in the pitch darkness beyond the fire. . . . I had taken one step toward the cave mouth when I heard it! The whispered crunch of feet in the sand!

I had the weird impression that the blackness around me had closed in, holding me like a strait jacket so that I couldn't move. I wanted to run, to hurl myself madly toward those creeping steps, meet whoever was coming and have it over with. But I couldn't budge, and the only motion of which I was conscious was my eyes swelling larger and larger in their sockets until they ached, while my eardrums strained to catch the grating of every grain of sand moved by those feet.

Closer, closer, so that the sound swelled in the darkness and I could tell the difference between heel and toe the feet came on. They were just beyond the bend of the cave. Then the madman stepped into the circle of light!

The force in my throat burst then, not

into a shriek but into the wild, hysterical laughter of relief. That horrible cachinnation jabbered and banged against the walls of the cave, rolled in furious, insane torrents into the darkness.

The idiot stood watching with his one good eye, while his scar-twisted mouth seemed to leer sympathetically. Finally, when my laughter had choked to a gurgle and I was on my knees beside the fire, he said: "So you thought I was Desis and you wouldn't be able to escape this time. No wonder you was glad to see me."

"Listen," I said. "Who in God's name are you? And who is she? How did you get here? What's happening here?"

"You don't know?" The eyeless socket peered at me like one of the skulls in the dark; the twisted mouth bent only on one side when he spoke.

"How in the devil could I know? A man in Mobile paid me to learn if a ship had wrecked here five years ago carrying pearls. I came across the swamp in a boat and got here tonight. That's all I know."

His mouth twisted in that hideous, one sided fashion. "I'm the last livin' one outa that ship's crew. Soma the others are around you." He gestured toward the dark where the skeletons lay. "She loved them, and killed them, and ate them."

I lunged half erect, shouting, "You're lying, lying! She couldn't have done that." Then, the words choking in my throat, I asked, "Who is she?"

His mouth twisted again. "Howda I know? She was here when I came. She says her name's Desis, and you say that's a spider. Maybe she is; maybe she's the daughter of hell. I thought at first she was just a cannibal woman. But she ain't human. I know that now!"

I HAD been thinking these very things, letting them grow on me until I was half mad with superstition and fear. But

when he put them into words it acted like cold water on me, and I began to fight again against the terror. I told myself that I was letting fear run away with me; that I had to keep a cool head, and think. But it was damned hard sitting there in that dark cave, with the firelight bringing out all the horror of the face across from me. I dug my fingers into my thighs, pulled every muscle in my body stiff.

"Listen," I said. "All this is a lot of tommyrot. Desis may be unusual, but she's human. There's no need for two men to be afraid of any woman."

He leaned toward me, the firelight running in a red flame along the scar that twisted his face. "You oughta know," he said. "You barely touched her, but from where I was hid I saw you jump and yell. You was damn lucky to get away. None of the others ever did. She loved them, and then she'd bite into their necks and then—" His face convulsed horribly.

"Why didn't she bite you?" I shouted at him. "What are you doing here?"

"I asked you to kill me." He began to pant now, like a dog. "I want you to do it now. When we got wrecked here I had a broke leg. That's why one of 'em's bent like it is, so I can't run well. And my face was all cut up, too. I woulda died, but she saved me. She's been waiting for me to get well enough so she—she can—" He choked.

Without warning he was on his knees, reaching toward me and his voice had taken on that high, thin pleading. "You gotta kill me! Now! She'll take me soon! I'm not brave like the others! I don't wanta have her love, in spite of what she'll do to me afterwards!"

"I can't kill you. I left my gun back there."

"Do it with your hands," he whispered. "With a stick. Anything."

"Goddamnit!" I said. "If you're so

anxious to die, why don't you do it yourself? Why don't you go out into that swamp, or swim out into the gulf. There are moccasins on one side of this place and barracuda on the other. They'd get you."

"No. They won't touch you after—after she has."

"You're crazy!" Then, suddenly I remembered the sound of that snake slithering away from me when I ran into the swamp. A cottonmouth moccasin is more likely to strike than run, but this one. . . .

"You could die in the swamp, anyway," I suggested at last. "You could swim out and drown. Why don't you do that?"

"I don't know. I wanta die and yet—somehow I can't. Maybe it's because she won't let me. I tried to drown, but I couldn't right off, and then she came and got me. I tried goin' in the swamp, and she pulled me outa there too. Somehow I can't kill myself. I want you to do it."

I shook my head, swallowing hard. "I think you are crazy," I said. "I think I'm crazy, too, and that this whole night's some kind of dream. But crazy or not, I'm going to get out of it, and I'll get you out, too. I've been in tight places before, without turning yellow—and I'm not going to do it this time." I stopped talking, feeling the man's eyes on me.

He knew, and I knew, that I *was* afraid, horribly afraid, and trying to bolster my courage with words.

WITH early morning sunlight pouring down across the beach, I felt almost normal again. The knowledge that I was marooned on this narrow strip of coast stuck in the back of my head, but that was the sort of danger I was accustomed to and didn't fear. I had no doubt that I could escape in some way. With the sun warm against my skin, the fantastic terror of the night before seemed almost absurd.

From the beach at the mouth of the cave I could see, a half mile to the west, a black hulk protruding from the water. It was about a quarter of a mile from shore, and the way in which waves piled up there indicated a reef.

"Is that the wrecked boat?" I asked the one-eyed man, pointing.

His lips twitched, the old fear came back in his face. "That's her. She hit there five years ago and rolled part way over. That's her stern stickin' outa the water."

"Where are those pearls I was told about? Tell me where they are; I'll help you get out of here."

I never expected him to tell me. I didn't really believe in the story of the pearls, and wouldn't have expected him to tell me about them if they did exist. But he said quickly, fear growing in his face: "They're still on board, in that cabin, aft. But you can't get them."

I was suddenly tense, staring at him. Then the pearls were real! Within a half mile of me there was a fortune, for the taking. My breath began to come shallow and quick. "Why in hell can't I get them? I can reach that cabin some way."

The man's leathery, sunburned skin had turned a sickly yellow. He whispered, "You can reach the cabin but you—you can't get out again. Some of the others tried it. They none of 'em got out. Desis"— his voice slipped down to where it was barely audible—"she got all of 'em who went there."

His words would have frightened me the night before; they sent a strange, eerie tingling along my spine even now. But in the bright sunlight things looked differently. I was ashamed of the terror I had felt because of a woman, and I was determined to prove to myself that I had conquered fear. Besides, well—I was thinking of that fortune, mine for the taking, and the lust of it had got in my blood stronger than fright. I could almost feel the pearls between my fingers, and a wild procession of the things money could buy trooped through my imagination.

"Listen," I said, "I'm going out there and get those pearls. If you've lied to me about them, I'm coming back and answer that prayer to kill you."

A hopeless, pitiful look was in the man's distorted face. "You'll go out," he said. "Maybe you'll find the pearls. But you ain't comin' back."

"I'm coming back—with the pearls." I began to walk up the beach, almost running in my eagerness.

He stumbled after me, caught at my hand, jerked me around. "Don't go!" he screamed. "Don't go! Kill me first. Please. *Please!*" He went down on his knees, arms around my legs, keeping up that wild, frantic pleading.

. Fear struck back at me, dank and cold as a black fog rising in my stomach, closing dreadfully about my heart and lungs. The man was insane, I told myself desperately. If he really wanted to die, he would have managed to kill himself.

Then I thought of the skeletons lying in the dark cave and of the marks like human teeth that pointed their spinal columns.

"You said Desis was a kind of water spider," he gasped, clinging to me. "You can't dodge her in the water. Others tried it who could swim good. She'll get you out there!"

In that moment, if I could have had the flat-bottomed boat I would have gone blindly, frantically away without caring in which direction I poled, as long as the hellish spot was behind me.

But I didn't have the boat, and after a moment the sunshine took effect again. The horror evaporated from me, my heart began to beat normally again. Once more the thought of those pearls, and the wealth they would bring, was a hot lust in my veins. Perhaps I should say that I thought of Jenkins and my duty to him for sending me here, but I didn't. All I thought of was what my half of the fortune would amount to.

I slammed my hand against the cripple's chest, hurled him away from me. "Those pearls damn sure better be there," I said, turning and beginning to run along the beach.

Behind me I heard him sobbing. Then his voice raised in a high, thin shriek. "You said that name meant a water spider. In the water you can't—" My own curses drowned out the rest.

FROM that time on things happened so swiftly, plunging so straight down to their gruesome finish, that I had the impression of falling from some immense height, hurtling headlong, whirling over and over without the slightest ability to control myself, through clouds of horror and misery and hell.

Even as I was running along the beach, I knew that if I paused the fear would overcome me and I would turn back; so I kept going. At a point opposite the hulk of the small ship I stripped myself down to my shorts, then ran into the water, began to swim.

I swam to the ship and around it once, then tread water, looking at it. She was a small, two masted schooner which had hit the reef hard, running almost entirely over it. She was all under water except her stern which protruded some eight feet, barnacle encrusted, above the waves.

I went close, took a long breath and dived. The water was glass-clear, and once below the surface there was not much surf. I found that the hatch leading into her stern was open, then I came up for air. "It shouldn't be any trouble to go through that hatch and find the cabin and the pearls," I reasoned. "I can get air where she sticks above the water."

Sudden, eerie apprehension struck me. I didn't want to go into that ship! I didn't want the pearls! I wanted to turn and swim for shore, with a wild, explosive speed that would take me there faster than thought. The fear of the ship, of the darkness beneath it, and the things I might find in that darkness chilled me even more than the water I swam in. I knew that in another moment I would turn for shore; and so, frantically, I dived. Once under the water I got control of my nerves and muscles again, but the fear didn't leave me entirely.

I didn't have to go deep, yet the temperature of the water seemed to change sharply, becoming colder and colder. It was fairly bright at first, only the shadow of the ship being dark. I could see the hatch easily, and using the breast stroke and kicking scissors fashion, I went through it.

The light changed swiftly now, dulling to a thick, heavy murk in which it was almost impossible to see. I cursed myself for being without the underwater torch which I had brought from Mobile. I almost turned back; but I knew that once away from this ship I would never have the nerve to return. I forced myself to swim on.

Feeling along the bulwark I found a cabin door, looked through. It was too dark here to see anything, so I pushed away, let myself float upward. My head struck wood, and I felt along it until I came to an opening. Glancing upward I was conscious of greylight. I struck down with both hands, felt my body rising.

Something tapped my forehead lightly, swayed, and slipped along my face. It was sleek and hard and cold. At first I thought it was a fish. Then I felt it along the whole side of my face, and I *knew!*

I tried to scream, my mouth wide open and bubbles bursting out to roll past my ears with a sound like exploding shells. I thrashed the water, fighting to get out of there, but struggling blindly without any sense of direction.

For the thing which had touched on my face was a human bone!

Abruptly my head broke water. Tiny threads of mote-filled radiance made a grey gloom in the place, and I knew I was in the elevated stern cabin of the ship, the sunlight filtering between cracked planking. What had been the bottom of the 'tween deck sloped very gently down into the water. I crawled up on it, looked about and saw a built-in bunk where lay another of those headless skeletons!

There was a pile of blankets at one corner, an overturned table near the water's edge, a chair tilted back against the left bulwark. But I wasn't conscious of seeing those things. My eyes were on the blankets, straining against the gloom, swelling until they ached in their sockets. My mouth was open, twitching, but I made no sound.

Piled among the blankets were three disordered skeletons—*and the skull of each one had been severed from the spine!*

I went toward them, the way a bird may go toward a snake which has hypnotized it. I was half crouched, my fingers extended in front of me were both reaching for the bones. I already knew the way those skulls had been displaced, yet I could not keep myself from examining them, from the thought of what I would see. . . .

Slowly, my whole body trembling, I knelt, reaching out for the bones. But I never touched them, or if I did I can't remember. For it was in that second, hand extended, that I saw the pearls.

There was a great pile of them resting on the rotting blanket beside one of the skeletons, a bony hand of which seemed almost to cup them in fleshless fingers. For one moment I gazed at them, dazed and unbelieving, then shouting with hysterical joy, I scooped them up and almost buried my face in them. There must have been at least fifty—each absolutely alike —about pea-sized, and even in the dull gloom I could see the pink glow of them that was more delicate than a flower. I had a fortune in my two hands, a fortune beyond estimation.

I STOOD up, laughing, head thrown back and chest shaking. I had almost turned back with this wealth at my finger tips, because I was afraid of a woman. After the bone had touched my face under water it was blind fear which had sent me bursting into this treasure. "Afraid of a bone caught between two planks under water," I shouted. Tilting my cupped palms, I rocked the pearls back and forth, listening to the tinkle of them.

Gradually, my eyes still watching the pearls, I felt *her!*

I didn't look up, because at first I wasn't sure she was there. I wasn't sure of anything except a slow-growing fear that crawled like some black and ghostly fungus through my body, coiling with sickening pressure about my intestines, slipping up toward heart and lungs.

There had not been any sound in this place except the noise I made and the eternal lapping of water against the planks around me. There was a new tenseness, a strange tangible lack of other sound in the air, which made the water seem hungry and lustful and hideous.

My hands shook and the muscles in the back of my neck stiffened as I heard her voice saying, "Do you think the pearls are pretty? I hoped you would come for them."

I staggered backward on the sloping floor, cowered there, still holding the pearls in front of me, and looked at her.

She was in the water just beyond the point where the deck slid into it. Her breasts were half visible, the tawny golden flesh looking exotically white against the gloom. Her face was as beautiful as some savage orchid that lures life into death by its beauty. She made no attempt to hide her eyes now, and I could see the red, hellish flame of them, the unbearable, terrific glare that was like hot coals from hell pushed against my own eyeballs.

I must have stared into those eyes a full minute before I was able to shift my gaze, to notice her hair. It lay in a long, heavy silver mass that fell about the sides of her face and floated on the water. And although her breasts and shoulders glimmered wetly the water seemed never to have touched her hair! It was like a mass of silver spider webs, widespun and waiting for their victims.

"Aren't you glad to see me? You ran away last night." Without any evident motion she came closer to the edge of the deck, her breasts lifting higher from the water.

Mingling with the terror that had frozen me, passion came, slow and tremendous. I could feel it starting low in my body, heating my already taut muscles, setting a flame to lapping at my heart. With the desire came an overwhelming, furious terror that made me fight the desire more than I had ever fought fear; that set my whole body to trembling so that one of the pearls dropped from my shaking hands and rolled along the deck.

"I knew you would come for the pearls," she said. "I want you to have them, but"—with one graceful movement she was out of the water and standing, entirely nude—startling—and amazingly beautiful, on the edge of the deck—"you can have the pearls later," she whispered.

"I've been here so long—alone." She held her hands out to me.

Desire burned out the fear inside me then. One white wave of flame seemed to sear my body, to burn the woman's beauty into my soul as I went reeling toward her, mouth open with a quick intake of breath, desiring nothing but her body. It was unconsciously that I clung to the pearls.

"Take me—!" Her whisper throbbed in the narrow space as she came swiftly nearer. Her eyes blazed with passion, and her lips were pulled back wide from her teeth. One tiny stream of sunlight caught her face then, held it so for a split second, as if in the light of a torch.

For the first time I saw her teeth! They glittered white, long and needle sharp as those of a barracuda! Teeth that could sever a man's skull from his spine!

I MUST have screamed, for there was a splitting cacophony tearing at my eardrums, a shriek that drowned out the tinkling fall of the scattered pearls. With one terrific lunge I avoided her outstretched hands, leaped for the water. My foot skidded on the deck and I fell hard, rolled, clawed at the wood, then dived. In that half second while I was in the air, while my scream still shuddered through the place, I heard Desis laugh. It was the low and hideously confident laughter of the swamp.

And even as my hands found the underwater opening through which I had come, I heard the small sound she made in diving after me.

I'm a good swimmer, and with terror lashing me I must have gone swiftly. "I'll make it!" I thought. "I'll make it!" A dull light showed up ahead, and I knew that I was almost free of the ship. At that moment I felt her hand on my foot. Desperately I tore free, struck out again. But now her arms closed around my waist, pulling me down. I twisted toward her, doubling my fists. In the dim light I could see her face just below mine, feel her naked breasts flattened hard against me. I uttered a gasping, choked curse—and swung a powerful right at her jaw.

But my fist never landed. Something jerked it back, held it and, when I tried to strike with the left hand, it too was tied against my side. And then I went mad! It was her hair that had tangled around me, the way a spider web wraps about a fly!

I weighed a hundred and seventy and was in good condition. Madness added to my strength, and I fought as a sane human being could not fight. My whole body writhed and twisted, every muscle in me strained and tore in a cyclonic effort to break free of the woman's hair. But it was no use.

The fight went out of me. There was a grey twilight world under the water, and I was conscious of Desis pressed against me, of every voluptuous curve of her naked body and the sleek feel of her hair about my shoulders. There was no emotion in me except a dull desire for her, and my head tilted down toward her lips.

I MUST have lain quietly for some time after regaining consciousness, because when I first moved, and looked about me, most of my strength had returned. And with it had returned the passion and fear. But I knew, even from that first moment, that the passion would win this time and I was doomed.

I was lying far enough inside the cave for the darkness to merge with the sunlight reflected from the mouth into a dull semi-lucent greyness. Beside me, her body unbelievably alluring, was Desis, a few strands of her silver hair coiled around my shoulders. The rest was massed like a great pillow of spiderwebs below her head.

I moved, almost unconsciously, and the hair tightened, holding me beside her. She raised her head and smiled at me. "You almost drowned by acting so foolish. I had a hard time saving you."

For a moment her red eyes blazed lustfully into mine, sending mingled terror and passion boiling through my veins again, setting my muscles to twitching.

"Am I so ugly you'd rather drown than love me?" Her hand touched gently against my shoulder.

I knew what would happen if I loved her. I had seen the skeletons without heads. I'd heard the wild cry of the cripple, "She's killed them all! Eaten them!" I no longer doubted. I knew that he had told the truth, and I knew that once I had loved her I would be only one more moldering skeleton within the cave.

I fought, so help me God, I fought against the desire for her. But from the first I knew I couldn't win. She wasn't human, and the lust she stirred in a man was beyond human enduring.

"Am I so ugly?" she whispered again, both hands on my shoulders pulling me toward her. The white, pointed teeth gleamed between her lips, hungry and trembling; her red eyes burned like fire into mine. I rocked toward her; then, fighting with every muscle in my body, I stopped, though I could make no effort to pull away.

"You're not ugly," I panted. "You are beautiful, damnably, inhumanly beautiful." The words ached in my throat as I fought them out.

"Then why? Why do you not take me?" She kept pulling me gently toward her, and her hands seemed to burn into my flesh.

"It's because you'll kill me!" I was panting like a dog and my whole body hurt with wanting her. "You'll bite into my throat, take my blood. You did it to the others. You'll kill me, too!"

"Yes." She almost hissed the words, and the red lips trembled around her teeth; her eyes blazed. "But don't you want me—enough for that?"

I don't know how I managed it, but I made one last, terrific effort to pull away from her. Somehow every muscle in my body seemed to explode, in one furious backward lunge. I came to my knees, thought I was away!

Then the strands of hair that were like steel cords tightened around my shoulders, and I was jerked back against her; and, with the touch of her flesh, all resistance went out of me. I caught her fiercely against my chest. There was a bursting flame of wild passion that enveloped us, and through which I could not see. I heard her cry out, moan, but I could not see her because of the fire coming in with one last great wave, leaping into a final burst—then going completely.

IT WAS in that moment of utter emptiness that her teeth found my throat! I felt the parting of the skin, the hot spurt of blood and her lips against me. I went insane, screaming, trying to jerk up my fists and strike at her. But her hair tied me, and then there was no strength left in my muscles to struggle.

I have never remembered the beginning of the cry; perhaps I didn't hear it. But all at once, just over my shoulder, a man was bellowing, "By God this is how you should die, how I wanted to kill you! And now . . . !"

I managed to twist my head, feeling Desis's lips let go their suction grip on my throat, hearing the short gasp of fear that she made. And then I saw the man standing above me, saw the knife rip downward. I rolled to one side, still tangled in those few strands of Desis's hair.

How it happened after that, I can't say

exactly. The knife ripped at my shoulder, sliced through the restraining hair. Somehow I was on my feet, staring into the face of Jenkins, the man who had sent me to this place. He swung up the knife, came toward me slowly.

"You didn't know," he panted, "that I was Ann Bentley's husband. You didn't know that I sent you here so that I could kill you, without anyone learning of it. Even here you find a woman, but I'll—"

I turned and ran. Behind me I heard the short, terrible scream of Ann Bentley's husband—and then there was silence.

I found the boat in which he had come, and I left in it. I didn't look for clothes; I went just as I was. If you'll look in the Mobile papers for October some eight years ago, you'll find an account of the capture of a naked madman. But I wasn't insane. I just made the mistake of trying to tell the truth.

* * *

ED ROLAND stopped talking. He was still sitting with his back against the post, his long spider-like legs drawn up under him, arms wrapped around his knees. For a moment I looked at him.

"Are you trying to get me to believe that?" I asked at last.

He said, "No, I didn't think you would believe it. But it happened."

"You're crazy," I told him. "The only thing which could have happened is that Jenkins, or Bentley—or whatever his name was—sent you to that place in order to kill you, planted the man and woman there to frighten you first. But there's no sense to that, and it wouldn't explain the woman's eyes—and a lot of things."

"No," Ed Roland said calmly. "It wouldn't explain those things. It wouldn't explain why Ann Bentley's husband never came back to Mobile. And it wouldn't explain this . . . " He stood up, pulled open his shirt collar and stepped toward me.

A great circular scar such as teeth might make twisted one side of Ed Roland's throat.

THE END

THE
Red Eye of
Rin=Po=Che
A long novel by
NORVELL
W. PAGE

O'Moore gazed long into Death's red eye—and found the girl and the fight that his wild heart had been seeking. . . .

O'Moore laughed—and leaped to meet them.

CHAPTER ONE

Kiss of Death

THE SMILE on the girl's proud, red mouth was fixed, but her eyes darted everywhere like frightened small dark birds in a trap.

Across the table from her, the man was

smiling also, and the pupils of his eyes just showed beneath waxy lids, opaque and merciless as a cobra's.

"No," he said softly, "there is no escape. You must obey!"

On the dance floor at the girl's elbow, men and women swayed to the thumping of a swing band. Waiters glided noiselessly along the table aisles. All these were here in the Club l'Antique, and outside were the moiling streets of New York City—and she was as alone, as helpless as if she were a prisoner in the uplands of forbidden Nepal. The girl's eyes were slowly widening with that realization and they held the shine of terror. And still she smiled, and the man across from her smiled.

"There is no escape, save in obedience," he repeated, and triumph glistened in his slanted, Eastern eyes.

IN THE doorway of the Club l'Antique, O'Moore stood motionless and scowled. His broad shoulders and great height made him bulk above the other men who crowded past him; that and the arrogant way he carried his strong-boned head with its wavy black hair, and the challenging way his blue eyes thrust about him. O'Moore was bored with inaction, and his black mood was on him, and he knew of no reason at all why he should put up with this blaring noise that aped, but could not equal, the savagery of native drums he knew; or why he should tolerate these flaccid crowds, or the obsequious murmur of the headwaiter at his elbow:

"Your usual table, Mr. O'Moore, sir?"

O'Moore rolled his impatient shoulders beneath the perfect tailoring of his evening dress. "Must it always be the same table?" he growled testily.

But he followed the headwaiter—for he knew suddenly that this would be his last night in New York. It was palling on him again, as all cities did soon or late, and he'd be off half across the world on

some new adventurous quest. A man couldn't breathe in this great crowded city, much less find a fight—and O'Moore, with that black mood on him, needed a fight! A bloody fight, he told himself, with fists and chairs and bottles flying!

It was the way his thoughts ran when he passed the table where the girl fought with her smile against the trap she was in. O'Moore's bold blue eyes swept over her, and approved the fine thoroughbred lines of her body, and the proud way she carried her small dark head. He thought that if he knew a girl like her, New York might be tolerable! And her eyes lifted to his, and suddenly she was on her feet with a small cry!

"John! Oh, John!" she cried. "Where have you been!"

Then she flung her white smooth arms about O'Moore's neck, and kissed him on the mouth!

Now John wasn't his name and he didn't know the girl, but O'Moore, being the man he was, put his arms about the girl and kissed her back. Her lips were cold and trembling under his, and there was trembling throughout all her sweet body—and he remembered that there had been terror in her eyes, and in her set smile. O'Moore's eyes grew merry, and his heart lifted. The girl still clung against him and, her cheek soft against the weathered tan of his own, she was whispering in a dry and frightened voice: "Pretend you know me—and get me out of here quickly! My life is in danger!"

O'Moore reflected that would be only fair repayment for the kiss. He didn't know what the girl's game was. Things like this just didn't happen in New York. But whether this was some trick to rope in a sucker with money; or whether the girl was merely drunk, it didn't matter. He thought that he saw a chance for a fight!

O'Moore set the girl at arm's length from him, and smiled with his blue eyes.

"Sure, now, darling," he said. "Why did you run away from me?" he asked gently. "I knew I'd find you again, but why did you run away?"

It was not until then that he looked toward the girl's table, and the man seated there—and he felt a coldness then like that time in Bengali when he had stepped bare-footed from his cot, and felt the convulsive coils of a cobra beneath his naked sole! For he recognized the man at the table as one of those venomous crossbreeds that only the brown and yellow East can spawn! For the first time, then, O'Moore began to think that the girl's whisper might hold some grain of truth. For what was this lovely girl doing with this pariah? O'Moore felt anger stretch his mobile lips, and he put his hands on the edge of the table.

"Oh, come away, John!" the girl was pleading. "I have so much to tell you! Mr. Nachi won't mind, I'm sure."

There was nervousness in the girl's voice, but O'Moore's temper was stubborn.

"Thou pariah cur!" he said softly, in the Hindustani which is the *lingua franca* of all the brown East. "Take thy unclean self away! Only white men enter here!"

FOR an instant, the man's glittering eyes flared wide in surprise, then he snapped to his feet. Amid the spattering of applause as the dance music ended, the crashing of his chair was sharp and loud. But O'Moore saw his hand dart like a claw beneath his coat—and O'Moore did not move at all. Only the stiffened line of his lips curved in a waiting smile, and his blue reckless eyes weighed coldly on the masked gaze of the Eurasian.

The girl's hand was tugging at his arm again, and her whisper was insistent. "Oh, come away," she pleaded. "There are a score of them!"

O'Moore laughed. "Only twenty? Why, in the Khyber country, we reckon the proper odds one white man against forty such as this! Go, dog!"

His tone was contemptuous, but his eyes were watchful. These half-breeds could strike with the speed of cobras, especially when they smiled as this Eurasian was doing now, showing his yellow fangs. The man's hand swung into view, empty. He made a brief, too-servile bow.

"My master has spoken," his voice was sibilant, mocking. "The dog goes, but beware when the dog shall return."

He marched away toward the doorway and O'Moore watched him go with a sudden heavy frown. He was realizing suddenly that the girl must have spoken literal truth when she said her life was in danger! The breed was too cock-sure. Yes, there would be trouble ahead. . . . And suddenly, O'Moore threw back his head and let his rich laughter boom out. Well, he had been aching for a fight, hadn't he? And the girl was lovely to look at, and soft in his arms. Still laughing, he turned toward the girl—and an oath ripped from his lips.

The girl had vanished!

O'Moore's smile turned angry on his mouth, and his eyes shot about him fiercely. Now, what sort of game was this? With grim humor, O'Moore patted his pockets with careful hands. No, nothing had been stolen, and nothing planted on him, so it wasn't that sort of trickery. Then, what the devil? O'Moore's eyes were steady and cold. No man or woman played tricks with Moriarity Aloysius O'Moore with impunity. That was what he told himself, but in the back of his mind, or perhaps it was his heart, there was a spot of cold apprehension. Damn it, the girl hadn't been acting! She had been trembling with *terror!*

O'Moore's eyes were still questing over the dozens of couples filing toward their tables again and, abruptly, he spotted the proud high head of the girl, moving swiftly toward the main entrance! O'Moore began to plough through the dancers. Men glared toward him angrily, but one glimpse of his face silenced them. There was not even an oath of protest.

Once more, O'Moore stood in the entrance of the Club l'Antique, and the girl was nowhere in sight . . . but the yellow man was there, and there were two others with him. They stood in a close group by the cloak room. Their eyes reached out toward h i m i n n a r r o w hostility. O'Moore's teeth flashed white in his tanned face and he began to saunter toward them. His shoulders swung a little, easily, as an athlete's will, and his head was lifted so that the black slab of his hair was tossed off his high forehead. His blue eyes did not waver. He thought he could make these yellow devils sing a true song!

It was when he was a scant five yards away from the three, and they were swinging into a close wedge to confront him that he caught movement out of his eye-corners. . . . *The girl!* She was smiling brightly toward the yellow men, walking straight toward them—and she did not look toward O'Moore at all!

In a single, long stride, O'Moore reached her side. His solid fingers closed firmly on the softness of her arm.

"Just a minute, darling," he said gently. "There is a bit of explaining to do before you join your friends!"

The girl's eyes flung up to his, startled. "There must be some mistake," she stammered. "I'm afraid I do not know you!"

"Why, there's a fragment of truth in that," O'Moore agreed, and his tone was gay. "But a kiss makes us somewhat friends, even though strangers, and. . . ."

He broke off then as the girl wrenched her arm free and struck him stingingly across the mouth. "Let me go, you drunken lout!" she cried.

O'Moore stiffened under that blow, though the smile was fixed on his lips. She had stung him, the little devil, and

there was the taste of blood in his mouth. "As you say," he murmured quietly, "there doubtless is some mistake!"

THERE was no mistaking the hostility in the girl's eyes—and there was no slightest gleam of recognition in them. O'Moore turned stiffly toward the cloak room and recovered his silk hat and his cape, and his ivory-headed cane of ebony. His dignity took him out of the club; but his curiosity would not let him rest. Now, surely, there was some strange mystery here! Had the girl been threatened, meantime, that she turned on him so fiercely? What, in the devil's name, was all this about? O'Moore lifted the cane and tapped its carved ivory head against his chin. Now, by all the saints, no one was going to deal him out of the fun like this! He'd get to the bottom of it!

O'Moore turned back toward the club entrance—he had been standing, thinking, in the shadows beside the awning marquee —and he saw the girl once more. She seemed always to be flitting past his eye corners, though there was nothing furtive in her movements. O'Moore had a feeling that she was always going to be there like that, turning up when he least expected her, and always causing that little twinge in his heart. Pity, of course—for her head was carried so proudly, and she was riding for a fall!

He saw her signal to the doorman for a cab, and one spurted to the awning. O'Moore caught the frightened gleam of her eyes as she glanced toward the club, then she was climbing into the cab. For one instant, O'Moore hesitated. Then he laughed lightly . . . and leaped behind her into the cab! It would be worth another slap in the face!

The girl whirled toward him with a small, frightened cry, and her narrow white hands snatched for the dress-purse on her knees. Then she gasped, and relief made her voice break. "Oh, it's you! For a moment, I thought. . . ." Her voice trailed off and she sagged back against the cushions.

The cab lurched forward, nosed into the traffic of Fifth Avenue and O'Moore, studying the girl beside him, heard a sound that drew every nerve in his body taut and whipped him about violently in his seat. It was a sound that began as a low minor wail, like a thin siren in the distance, mounted terribly . . . and cut off with the suddenness of death at its highest point. It was like the hunting cry of some half-human beast! O'Moore stared fixedly behind them on the street, for it was a devilish thing to hear here in the midst of New York City. In the highlands of Tibet, a man might expect such a thing. . . . Beside him, the girl was shuddering.

O'Moore wiped the startled frown from his brow and made his voice light as he sought to calm the girl. "It sounds as if the yellow dogs were disappointed, darling."

The girl's face was white and strained as she turned her dark eyes upon him. "Oh, you must leave me," she said. "You must!"

O'Moore laughed, an ' 't was partly at the tartness of his own nerves. "Sure now, darling," he said. "You can't kiss a complete stranger, then slap him in the mouth and run away without a word! That sort of thing really isn't done—not with Moriarity O'Moore!"

"Slap you?" the girl whispered. "I didn't. . . . Oh, what does it matter? Don't you understand that you are in danger?"

O'Moore's smile widened, "Never in greater," he agreed equably. "Ever since I looked into those dark eyes of yours. . . ."

"This is serious!" the girl cried. "Those men. . . . Oh, I wouldn't have asked your help if there had been any other way!"

"Scarcely complimentary," murmured O'Moore.

"If you leave me now," the girl ignored his jest. "I don't think they'll bother you again. But if you insist on going with me, there is no escape!"

CHAPTER TWO

The Beast's Cry

O'MOORE shook his head and the puzzled light in his eyes deepened. "This isn't a stage melodrama, you know," he said, and there was a touch of concern in his voice. "If you're playing some game with me. . . ." It was just the way the girl talked, of course, but he had a feeling that hostile eyes were watching him. Then that scream in the night, like the howl of a wild beast!

"What the devil is this all about?" he demanded with sudden sharpness.

The girl shrank back in her corner. "I can't tell you," she whispered. "I dare not tell you. It would be all your life was worth, for if I told you. . . ."

"Yes?"

"No, no, I cannot!" She leaned toward him, her eyes earnest and pleading, her white hand small on his arm. Soft white gloves were about her wrists, but her hand was bare—and lovely! "Just believe me — and leave me." She smiled, with a small trembling of her lips, and he saw that there was a dimple at the corner of her sweet mouth, and that just beside it was a tiny dark mole like a beauty mark. "A kiss got you in this trouble," she said hesitantly. "If I kiss you again. . . . Oh, will you please, please go? Believe me, it is for your own sake!"

O'Moore glanced over his shoulder. There did not seem to be anyone following but that feeling of being watched persisted. He smiled at the girl, touched his chin with the head of his cane.

"You raise a fine point," he said gaily. "Not to undervalue your kiss, my darling, but I have been bored these many weeks—and you ask me to deal myself out of the fun !"

"Oh, you fool !" the girl's voice was scornful. "These men *kill !*"

She was leaning toward him, and O'Moore made his decision. He believed now in this girl, and in her peril—though he could not guess the nature of the thing that threatened . . . and he knew that he could not leave her to face it alone. But his tone remained light, and her face was very close. The serious compression of her lips made the dimple come and go. He sighed and took her two shoulders in his hands.

"I was ever a fool for a dimple," he said, and kissed her—then winced as something hard and forceful that was surely the muzzle of a gun, jabbed violently into his belly !

"Now, go !" the girl spoke with difficulty because of her quickened breath. "Go, before it's too late !"

Yet, O'Moore was positive that she had welcomed his kiss; that her lips had responded to his own !

He glanced down and saw that it was a gun in the girl's fist, a neat and deadly automatic, and her grip upon it was wholly competent. He looked back to the girl's eyes. "I think it already too late," he told her softly. "I have eyes in the back of my head, and they tell me that we are being followed !"

The girl gasped, threw a quick glance over her shoulder, and her pallor deepened before she whipped back toward him with an involuntary tightening of her gun hand. But O'Moore hadn't moved at all.

"Sure, now," he said gently. "I don't have to play tricks to take that gun away from you ! You wouldn't shoot me, you know. And we are being followed, aren't we ?"

"There's a car," the girl acknowledged, her voice tight with strain. "Oh, please, please. . . ."

O'Moore had that curious smile on his lips and he was twisting the ivory head of his cane. He lifted it a bit from the ebony stick so that a slim shaft of metal showed between. "I'm quite sure there is going to be a fight," he said, "and it's what I've been wanting these weeks past ! I'll deal with these yellow beggars while you call the police. In case we should become separated. . . ." O'Moore drew out a card case and scribbled the address of his club upon its back. "Moriarity Aloysius O'Moore," he murmured. "The Mogul Club. Very much at your service !"

The girl's fingers trembled as O'Moore closed them over the card. "You can still get away," she pleaded. "If anything happened to you, I'd. . . ."

O'Moore leaned toward her, "Yes?" he whispered.

BEFORE her trembling lips could frame an answer, the whine of speeding tires was suddenly loud beside the taxi. With a rigid arm, O'Moore swept the girl hard back against the cushions seat. He heard the taxi driver curse just while he braced his feet against the front before the shriek and crash of colliding metal made a deafening racket within the taxi. The cab swerved wildly, took the curb in a pounding leap and swung broadside under the driver's frantic hands.

"Steady, my dear," O'Moore whispered. The girl's head was locked hard against his shoulder, but both their straining faces were turned toward the heavy car racing beside the taxi. From the windows peered the inimical yellow masks of the Eurasians. The sedan was closing in again. . . .

The shock as the taxi slapped sideways into the wall wrenched O'Moore over in his seat and he carried the girl with him, but his hard-braced legs held firmly. The taxi caromed, slithered sideways—and the pursuing car rammed it, broadside !

The driver screamed. O'Moore saw his hands wrench high above his head in agony. Broken glass was flying like sharp glistening knives. Then a second impact as the taxi caught a light pole spilled O'Moore to his knees on the floor!

In an instant, O'Moore was up, but he pressed the girl to the floor. "Sit you there, darling," he said softly—and flung wide the door! He leaped to the pavement, sword cane in his fist, and slammed the door shut behind him. Quick as he was, the yellow men had been faster!

There were six of the breeds, spilling from their car, and each one carried a long bladed knife in his fist! O'Moore's lips quirked back from his teeth. Knives, of course! They wouldn't want the police yet awhile! His heart beat quickly and hard in his chest, and there was wariness in the shift of his eyes. Close quarters, and six men against him. . . . Faith, it was long odds, even for Moriarity Aloysius O'Moore!

O'Moore's hands met on the cane, ripped apart . . . and steel whined from the ebony scabbard! "Come on, you yellow dogs!" O'Moore taunted them. "Steel against your steel, and maybe a sliver now and then for your yellow hearts!"

For an instant, the ring of yellow men sagged back before the menace of that shining sword, expertly poised in his right hand, and O'Moore's eyes flicked over the street. They had swung into a side street in the upper sixties and, half a block away, the big buses and sleek traffic slipped by on Fifth Avenue. Here, there was darkness and the haughty facades of wealthy private homes that showed only a few slim gleams of light. The two cars had jammed together at an angle and it was in that angle that O'Moore waited, silk hat upon his head, the cape gallant about his shoulders and his sword raked out before him.

To an extent, the narrow opening was a help, but if they came at him through the car beside him, it would be bad. It would be very bad for O'Moore—and the end for the girl!

These thoughts were a flicker across his brain while the line of assassins swayed back from the first glinting menace of his sword . . . then the six swayed forward to the attack, and there was no time for thought at all!

O'Moore's swift glance swept over the faces of the men and found that the girl's escort, Nachi, was not among them. It was a curious thing that there was not a single pure racial type among them. Scum of the East, they were, and privy to all its vices and viciousness—but they wielded the knives like experts! They came in slowly, all together, the knives low against their thighs, shoulders rolled forward so that all the power and weight of their agile bodies would go into every thrust. The man on the extreme right of the attacking line drew back his arm a merest fraction and O'Moore's lips tightened. Years in the East had taught him the significance of that gesture, the preparation for the throw!

IT CAME an instant later and, at the same time, the others leaped forward with sharp, wild cries! O'Moore laughed —and leaped to meet them! The cane in his left hand swung in a sharp arc, caught the flying knife in mid-air and slammed it, ringing, against the side of the taxi. In the same split-instant, his sword raked out—and one curse was cut off in midnote! Before the man could slump to the pavement, O'Moore had leaped sideways and, with a quick stab of the blade, laid low the man who had thrown the knife. Then he was back in his angle, with only four of the killers before him!

In the face of such deadly execution, the men shrank back, and O'Moore flung back his head and sent his deep laughter ringing to the vault.

"Ha, dogs!" he mocked them in their native tongue. "Did you think to cut down a helpless doe? Come again, and feel the sharp prick of my horns!"

He could hear the hissing breath of the four men and they came in more cautiously a second time, but without shrinking. A hat, snatched from a man's head, sailed straight at O'Moore's face. O'Moore's cane plucked it from the air . . . and his sword still waited. The line of attack paused once more. It was the moment for which O'Moore had waited.

With a shout that was between laughter and a curse, he leaped forward! The quick play of his sword was like flickering light. The singing note of steel on steel rang through the narrow confines of the street. A man leaped back, cursing in a high shrill voice with his knife-hand broken! Another sagged to the pavement, strangling on his own blood! Victory was within O'Moore's grasp—and he slipped! He went down on one knee, and triumph shrilled in the shouts of the two men who remained on the offensive. They came in on him together, from two sides, and they were no longer hampered by the close pressure of their companions. One of them, O'Moore thrust back with a sharp blow of the cane; the other avoided his point and leaped past it with a striking knife!

Frantically, O'Moore flung himself backward and up—and was caught in his own trap! The tangled fenders of the two cars struck him across the back of the knees and his hands whipped up, his back bowed at the impact! In the same instant, the two men were upon him! No time to bring the sword down in a clean thrust. O'Moore flicked it from his hand like a javelin and its keen point slashed into the cheek of the nearer man, but it had no force behind it. The man staggered—and the flame of gun-powder lanced from the door of the taxicab!

In that taut moment, all action seemed to take place in slow motion. O'Moore saw the loom of the girl's white face in the doorway of the taxicab, saw the bullet-hole punch blackly in the temple of the man who had taken the sword in his cheek. The head wrenched over brokenly, the knife hand flew upward like a stiff arm-signal, and the right leg lifted also from the earth. Then the man's body whirled slowly about and the knees sagged. His nose bounced off the running board of the sedan, and he turned again. Wind gusted from the man's mouth like a sigh and his legs and arms jerked a little as he stretched out on his back on the earth. The sword waved like a reed, still embedded in the man's cheek.

O'Moore was conscious of these things while he fought for balance, while he fought to strike out at the second in-leaping knife-man. He knew that the girl could not bring her gun into play in time for a careful shot—because he himself was in her direct line of fire! And he caught the bitter gleam of the knife as it slashed in for his belly in a ripping stroke, edge turned terribly upward. O'Moore's muscles would not co-ordinate, would not move swiftly. Or perhaps they only seemed to react slowly. He jerked down the tip of the cane and, with his left arm still high above his head, jabbed it forward. There was no force in the blow, but the point was toward the assassin's eyes, and the man ducked his head a little as he came in.

O'Moore felt the shock of the man's knife-fist against his hip, and he laughed between locked teeth. Was he to take his death here there in this narrow alley of a city that . . . that bored him? Too soon to know whether the knife had hurt him badly. Too soon . . . but a fury seized O'Moore. He brought his right hand down in an awkward hammer blow atop the man's head, brought up his left knee violently. He heard the hissing wail of the pain of that double blow, and he bowed his body forward, bearing the man to earth. Now he could get some force into his cane. He twisted it in his hand and gripped it like a blunt-tipped knife, struck the ferrule straight down into the back of the man's neck!

All his body's weight, and all the strength of his broad shoulders went into that savage stroke!

RESISTANCE went out of the man bent double beneath him and they pitched to the pavement together. O'Moore let go on the cane, caught himself on spread hands and whipped his feet upward. With a violent exertion of strength, he tossed himself in a handvaulting somersault, twisted in the air and came down on his feet facing toward the sprawling man. He was a little off balance and reeled backward two short steps before he could catch himself. The assassin did not even shudder. And the black ebony cane, with its metal ferrule, jutted straight upward from his neck like a lightly planted *espada* in the neck of a bull. But it had penetrated deeply enough. Without investigation, O'Moore knew that the man was dead!

O'Moore whirled, looked stiffly about him. He remembered that one man had suffered only a broken hand, but that man had fled. Of the others, not one remained on his feet. Truly, it had been a grand fight! O'Moore remembered then the shock of a blow in his hip and clapped a hand there. He found a tear in the cloth, a thin dribble of blood, but no more. The knife had only grazed him! O'Moore's breath came fast between his locked teeth and, moving toward the car, he reeled a little uncertainly. The fight had been fierce and furious and it had taken more out of him than he thought. He heard the thin wailing of a police siren in the distance, and he swore softly.

"My lady," he said, and his tone was light. "Your champion has triumphed— and now he claims his meed from the queen of love and beauty! Mount my

charger, and let's get the hell away from here!"

O'Moore laughed and swept open the door of the taxi—and then he swore incredulously.

The cab was empty—the girl had vanished again!

For a blank moment, O'Moore stared in fright about the street, but there was no sign of a struggle . . . and he saw that the girl had left him voluntarily after that shot which had saved his life. On the floor of the cab was one of her soft fragrant gloves—and on the window of the cab was a message, written in the red of a lipstick that was bright like blood.

"I can bring you only death," said the delicate letters of her script, then pitifully: "Forgive me . . . Aloha."

O'Moore laughed softly, and caught up the fragrant glove, and then his whole body jerked taut and he whipped about with his hand tense upon the sword cane. Once more, wailingly, he heard the cry which had signaled their departure from the club. The scream that was, terrible, like the cry of a wild beast!

CHAPTER THREE

Murder!

THE first police car rocketed into the street with a dying wail of its siren that was strangely reminiscent of that strange cry. The two uniformed men leaped to the pavement with drawn guns in their hands, stared in amazement at the bodies strewn upon the pavement. There was only one living soul visible, and that was a stupid-seeming man in full evening dress who leaned upon an ivory-headed cane and gaped at them through a monocle that gave his face a vapid air.

"Devil of a thing, what?" he said adenoidally. "Men carving each other up and one thing and another in the public streets. You bobbies should be more on the alert, what, what? Now in Lunnon, we do things a spot differently. . . ."

One of the cops stalked up to him stiffly. "What happened here?" he demanded. "Who are you?"

O'Moore looked at him through the monocle deliberately. "Devil a question to ask a man," he said plaintively. "Obviously some Eastern Johnnies have been killing each other. Just out for a stroll, donchaknow, and I stumble on bodies strewn upon the thoroughfare!"

The cop shoved forward his chin belligerently. "Now then, talk English, damn you! Who are you?"

"Your manners need mending, my good man," O'Moore said, while he fumbled in his pocket; drew out some papers. "Passport, what? Diplomatic immunity, that sort of thing. You can find me at the Mogul Club. Yes, thank you. And a good evening to you, officer."

O'Moore could stroll away presently at a pace that seemed casual and yet covered ground at an extraordinary rate. There was no diplomatic immunity attached to his passport, but his manner had completely overawed the policeman. They could reach him presently at the Club Mogul if they wished—and they would, damn them!

O'Moore spent the next two hours hunting for the girl, but he learned nothing at all. The Club l'Antique knew nothing of her, nor of the yellow men who had long since gone; there was nothing to be learned from the taxi men at the nearby stand and finally O'Moore had no choice except to return to his club and hope against hope that the girl would communicate with him there. How slim a chance that was he hated to consider. Furthermore, it was likely the police would be waiting. . . .

From the shadows across the street, O'Moore studied the street before the sombrely dignified facade of the Club Mogul, but could find no trace of watchers. He crossed rapidly then, ran up the brownstone steps. The lobby had its usual reserved quiet, a place of shadows and leather chairs that seemed wrinkled with their age and repressed by the traditions of the political background of the Mogul. Only a single unobtrusive bellhop in the shadows was in evidence, and the clerk, precise in formal attire, bowed stiffly behind the desk as O'Moore moved warily forward.

"Any mail?" O'Moore asked, and felt that there was strain in his voice. "Or any messages?"

The clerk laid a neatly wrapped square box on the counter, placed his hands on the edge of the marble slab and smiled vacantly.

"Only this, Mr. O'Moore," he said. "It arrived by messenger a short while ago."

O'Moore felt his heart thrust strongly and he could not keep down the smile that lifted his mouth corners. He could not mistake that handwriting in the address, though he had seen it only once before in the uncertain medium of lipstick. *Aloha!* But there was no return address on the package. He reached for it, and was a little surprised at the casualness with which he could do it.

"What messenger service was it, did you notice?" he asked softly.

"Why yes. The usual telegraph boy, sir."

O'Moore had the package in his hand and it seemed to burn his palm, but he must have the privacy of his room to open this. He swung away toward the elevators, heard the clerk speak again.

"Also, sir," he said, "the trunk was delivered to your chambers."

"The trunk?" O'Moore snapped; then he caught himself up. Probably that, too, had come from Aloha, but why in heaven's name? "Ah, yes, the trunk," he murmured. "I had forgotten." His eyes stabbed once more toward the street in precaution, and his fist tightened about the ivory head of his cane. Directly opposite the doorway, plainly visible in the white pool of a street light, stood one of the yellow men!

O'MOORE did not check his march toward the elevators, but the instant he was out of the yellow man's line of vision, he doubled toward the door and his stride lengthened out. His hands met on the sword cane, and a little wrench would free the slim, deadly blade! He had tokens from Aloha, but that absence of an address upon the box could mean only that she had no intention of revealing her whereabouts. He didn't know where to find her . . . but that yellow man would know! O'Moore's cleft chin thrust forward and his keen blue eyes were narrowed. Trunk and package must wait until he found out something about Aloha. And if that yellow man refused to talk . . . O'Moore's jaw locked ruggedly.

He was passing the brownstone column that flanked the front door of the club when a voice spoke sharply from the shadows.

"Don't move, O'Moore, *sahib*," the man said softly, "or I shall fill you full of nice round holes!"

O'Moore stopped in mid-stride beside the column. The yellow man across the street was no more than a vanishing shadow in a dark doorway—and he knew that the man had deliberately shown himself to draw him from the club! O'Moore cursed himself for his unwariness. In Peiping that trick would not have fooled him for a moment, but he had forgotten with whom he dealt! The mistake might well prove fatal! Out of his eyecorners, he could see the man who had challenged him. In his hand, a gun caught evil glints of light and his body was hidden in the blackness beside the thick marble pillar.

"You are wise, O'Moore *sahib*, to obey," the voice came again sibilantly. "I will relieve you of that small package you

just received! It is in your left hand. Hold it behind you. And mind you obey to the letter, O'Moore *sahib*—or the dog will tear his master to shreds!"

O'Moore's lids drooped over his eyes. He knew that he had no chance at all of whirling and striking before the man started shooting, yet there were hot, joyful lights in the hidden eyes of Moriarity O'Moore.

He made his voice shake as though with fury. "You have the advantage of me now, but my turn will come. . . ."

"Hold the package b e h i n d you, O'Moore. Quickly!" the man commanded arrogantly.

O'Moore's hand shook as he twisted it behind his back with the package balanced on his palm. He mouthed threats in a voice hoarse with futile anger, and the yellow man laughed sibilantly. He glided forward a step, the gun ready, his left hand reaching for the package. The trembling of O'Moore's hand became more violent—and the package fell to the stone steps!

The gunman leaped back as if he had been struck, but his laughter came again. "A child's trick, O'Moore," he said contemptuously. "Now, you will pick it up and hand it to me, and you will do it quickly, for my patience wears thin!"

O'Moore was a dejected figure as he turned about. The cane in his left hand seemed awkward and in his way. But O'Moore's eyes remained hidden and there was a laughter that pumped at his chest. He was facing the gunman now. He was bent stiffly forward, fumbling for the package—and his silk hat fell off. He swore, caught at it . . . and the cane flew from his left hand like a javelin, straight at the man's eyes!

At the same instant, O'Moore released the coiled springs of his leg muscles and hurled himself upon the yellow man. As he dodged aside, thrusting out the gun to fire, O'Moore's left hand clamped down hard on the chamber and bound it so that the gun could not be discharged. His right fist traveled six inches, smacked against the man's jaw and drove his skull back against the stone of the pillar! The Eurasian's hat bounced from his head and trundled down the steps. His gun slipped from his fingers and his body slumped forward limply into O'Moore's arms!

O'Moore pivoted, the gun reversed into his hand and ready, the man's body a shield before him, but there was no movement in the watching shadows across the street. In an instant, O'Moore pocketed the small white package, caught up silk hat and cane—and lugged the Eurasian into the lobby of the Club Mogul!

"Beggar tried to hold me up," O'Moore said casually to the staring clerk. "No, don't call the police just yet. I want to question this chap. There may be something political behind it!"

Those were magic words in these halls, where international politics were commonplace. The clerk bowed formally, and said nothing more as O'Moore marched toward the elevators. The cage lofted him swiftly to the twentieth floor where he had his suite. He dropped the unconscious yellow man to the floor, stood glaring down at him while his hands fumbled rapidly with the package which Aloha sent him. The paper peeled off and he saw a message scrawled on its inner face.

"Keep this, please, for me. You are good and kind, and I have no friends. Keep it, until I come."

O'Moore's forehead creased in a quick frown. He threw another glance at the man on the floor, opened the small box—and a startled cry rose to his lips! All the subdued light of the room seemed to concentrate inside the small box in his hand, which threw it back in coruscating gleams of scarlet! What he held was the most enormous ruby he had ever beheld in his life—and he had seen the great Forbidden Ruby, Aligar of Nepal!

WHEN his dazed brain could function again, O'Moore realized that he understood many of the things that had happened this night. The East attached religious significance to all its famous jewels, and surely this was one of the greatest! In God's name, what had Aloha to do with such matters! And how had this great jewel come into her possession! O'Moore whipped toward the door, fancying he caught some sound there; stared toward the windows. Better than many men, he knew the value of this stone and the danger its possession could bring. Murder was the least he could expect from these yellow assassins! It might have been imagination, but from the darkness beyond the window he thought he caught once more the bestial scream that twice before this night had heralded terror!

O'Moore tucked the stone into his pocket and bent swiftly over his prisoner. The man was still completely unconscious but he must be bound before he recovered. O'Moore had not lied when he said he intended to make him talk! With long strides that no longer held anything casual, O'Moore crossed the quietly rich drawing room. He had no means of knowing when or how the next blow would fall, but he knew without any doubt that it would come swiftly! God alone knew where Aloha was. She must have been in desperate danger to send this ruby by ordinary messenger to a complete stranger. Even though she had twice kissed that same stranger!

That smile was gentle on his strong face, but it stiffened into amazement—and caution—as he entered his bed chamber. He had forgotten the trunk the clerk mentioned, and it bulked huge in the shadows at the foot of his bed, seeming to squat there with menace. It was, his narrowing eyes told him, large enough to hold such men as these yellow devils—and he had no guarantee that it had come to him from Aloha!

O'Moore bounded into action. First his prisoner! His powerful hands shredded a thick turkish towel. He doused it with water and raced back to bind the yellow man tightly. Afterward, he returned to the trunk and switched the direct beams of a small reading lamp upon it. A close inspection showed no signs that it could be opened from within, no hint of ventilation holes. But before he made his decision concerning it, there would be wisdom in a search of his apartment! O'Moore did a thorough job of that and discovered someone else had been ahead of him. His high priced camera had been taken apart, a roll of valuable films ruined, and even his flashlight powders, which he still preferred to flash bulbs, had been emptied out. Searching for the ruby, of course. O'Moore's hands brushed the pocket into which he had thrust it, and he turned grimly back to the trunk.

With the captured revolver tautly ready in his fist, he loosened the fastenings and flung up the lid!

No sound at all passed O'Moore's lips then. His eyes strained wide, and pain struck through them. Something vital seemed to go out of his face, and the animation was sucked from his body as if by a sponge. He swung, reeled away and bowed his head against the wall. Through long minutes, he stood like that and then his head lifted rigidly and his face was white and stiff with a consuming anger. Even so, there was a fierce reluctance that seemed to fight against his movements as he walked heavily back to peer down again at the pitiful contents of the trunk.

He said, brokenly, "Aloha!"

Then he forced himself to bend closer over the trunk and look at the girl's body, cramped into that brutal casket—and he saw how she had died. It had been quick at least, for the bullet had drilled her squarely through the heart. The dark eyes were staring up blindly and there was

horror in the drawn lines of the mouth, and her white fists knotted tightly together. Poor little fists, that had touched his hand so fearfully, and . . . O'Moore ripped out an oath, and his eyes tightened. The girl had a glove on each wrist!

O'Moore's hand jerked to his vest and pulled out the glove he had found on the floor of the taxi, and then he looked more closely at the girl in the trunk. That mole like a beauty mark by her dimple. . . . By the heavens, this girl had none there! Only slowly then, the truth thrust into his dazed mind. This girl was not, could not be, Aloha!

His mind flashed back to the scene at the Club l'Antique. He closed his eyes, thinking hard, remembering every detail of the moment when he had accosted the girl and she had slapped him. Slowly, a smile built about his solid lips. There could be no doubt about it. The girl who had slapped him at the club had not been Aloha, but this girl! Undoubtedly, she was Aloha's sister, perhaps her twin. But it was not Aloha!

It was only when he knew this certainly that he could begin to think of the meaning of this girl being sent so secretly to his room; beyond any question, it meant that the yellow men intended to frame him for her murder, and. . . . His thoughts broke off with an oath. Faint at first, but growing rapidly nearer, he heard the shrieking of police sirens! He stared blankly down at the corpse of the murdered girl, a fierce menace to him now, and then his hand brushed his vest pocket where rested a ruby worth a king's ransom—and a dozen lives!

CHAPTER FOUR

The Yellow Men Come Back

THERE were three of the police cars and they skated to a halt before the Club Mogul. Men in blue uniform leaped from them, and there was one in civilian clothing who raced first up the brownstone steps.

"Lieutenant Davis, of Homicide," he snapped at the clerk. "Get your keys and take me to the room of Moriarity O'Moore! Fast!"

The clerk started to stammer a protest and Davis reached across the counter with a red hairy fist and grabbed him by the coat lapels. "I said, *fast!*" he repeated, sharply.

The elevator was swift and noiseless, and the carpeting on the twentieth floor was soft. The clerk pointed a shaking hand toward O'Moore's door . . . and, beyond that door, a gun began to blast! Shots ripped out in rapid sequence, sending their vibrant thunder through the hallway, and Lieutenant Davis swore in a high querulous voice and leaped toward the door. He jammed the key into the lock and, gun in hand, flung the door wide.

He stood staring then, and the clerk and the uniformed men crowded close around his shoulder.

There were three bodies stretched upon the floor, two men and a girl. The big man in the smoking jacket, stem of a big pipe thrusting up from the pocket, Davis spotted instantly as O'Moore. He lay sprawled on his face. His right temple, turned upward, had the bloody burn of a grazing bullet across it. The girl, queerly huddled against a divan, was dead with a wound over her heart. The Eastern-looking man, with a gun in his fist, had plainly been knocked out by the lamp vase whose shattered fragments lay about him on the floor—but knocked out too late to save the girl!

The tableau at the door held only an instant, then Davis leaped into the room, flung a command over his shoulder.

"Get cuffs on that yellow murderer!" he snapped. "Get a doctor up here, if there's one in this dump!"

He went down on his knees beside O'Moore and just then, the big man began to stir. He flung out his arms, fought to get to his feet. His wavy black hair sprawled across his forehead and his lips twisted with unintelligible sounds.

Davis held on to him. "It's all right, man. I'm Lieutenant Davis of the police!"

IT WAS only then that O'Moore seemed to get his eyes open. He looked about him wildly—and then all the fight went out of him. He looked down at the dead girl on the floor, moved heavily to a chair and sagged into it with his head between his hands.

"My sister," he said thickly. "She'd just come to see my rooms and that man. . . . He tried to hold me up outside the club. I knocked him out, brought him up here to question him. He must have been shamming unconsciousness, grabbed his gun. . . ."

Lieutenant Davis stood with hairy fists on his hips and glared down at the unconscious gunman, estimating positions, peering about for bullet scars on the walls. He took a step toward the girl, and O'Moore was watching him between his fingers, cupping his face. Abruptly, O'Moore leaped to his feet!

"By God," he muttered thickly, and his face was suffused with rage—a man could accomplish that by holding his breath. He staggered toward the unconscious Oriental. "By God, I'll finish him. I'll. . . ." He lifted his heel above the Eurasian's face as if to grind it to a pulp!

Davis reached him in a long leap. His big hands clutched O'Moore's shoulders, and his weight drove O'Moore aside.

"Cut it out, O'Moore," he growled. but his voice held rough sympathy. "We'll take care of him for you, and he'll pay. He'll pay plenty! Mike," he addressed one of the uniformed men, "take Mr. O'Moore to another suite. The clerk will open one for you. Stay with him, Mike."

O'Moore walked with an almost drunken passivity from the room and Davis sucked in a slow breath and turned once more toward the girl. He bent over her and caught sight of the edge of a slip of paper, tucked into her bodice beneath a lifted hand. He touched the hand gently, frowned at its coldness, and found that he had to use force to lift it from the paper! Damned funny business. Rigor mortis already? It didn't make sense, unless. . . .

Davis's eyes came to sharp focus on the slip of paper he had removed from the girl's bodice.

"I have been threatened," he read slowly. "If any harm comes to me, the man responsible will be Moriarity O'Moore!"

Davis read the message a second time and his eyes grew narrow and hard. He stooped deliberately over the girl again and tried the flexion of arms and knees. No doubt now about rigor mortis. This girl had been dead long before those shots were fired in this room! Sharply, Davis swung toward the door. His hat was pulled down over his brows, and the line of his jaw was ugly. He went with sharp, savage strides across the corridor toward where another door swung open. He peered inside, then he swore and leaped

to where the policeman, Mike, was stretched upon the divan comfortably. Mike was alone in the room, and there was a small dark bruise on Mike's jaw, and on Mike's chest was a calling card.

Davis snatched up the card. On one side, in neatly engraved letters, was the name, Moriarity Aloysius O'Moore. On the other side had been pencilled a single word:

"Sorry!"

TWO blocks away, O'Moore's taxi raced across traffic and O'Moore sat tautly forward with his fists knotted savagely on his knees. There was a grim hardness in the set of his jaw and he lifted a hand to finger the bullet-crease across his temple. His head still ached damnably. It had taken close calculation and an utterly steady hand to send that bullet at just the right angle past his own head. And there had been so damned little time . . . but there had been no other way.

At his curt order, the taxi swerved to the curb beside a cigar store and, a few moments later, O'Moore was back in the cab again . . . and now he knew from what address Aloha had sent him the package! She had overlooked the fact that the messenger service would keep a record of the errand.

"Washington Hotel," O'Moore snapped at the driver. "And there's an extra fiver if you can get some speed out of this truck !"

The cab writhed through traffic like a snake, raced through changing lights, and O'Moore sat rigidly braced and waiting. In a few minutes now, he would either be face to face again with Aloha—or he would learn of tragedy! It had seemed unwise to bring the ruby with him, and it was hidden in his rooms at the Mogul. If the police found it, they would keep it securely for Aloha. But he did not think they would find it! Meanwhile. . . .

The taxi cut to the curb before a quiet, old-fashioned hotel on a private park. O'Moore flung a bill at the driver.

"Wait !' he ordered and took the steps to the Washington Hotel in a single long bound. The door banged under the slap of his fist, and a sleepy night-clerk lifted his head from his book-keeping.

"Send my name to room forty-seven !" O'Moore snapped. "Moriarity O'Moore !"

The clerk shook his head slowly. "A sad thing," he said. "I hope you can help her . . . Miss Martin was taken suddenly ill and taken to the hospital not half an hour ago, sir. She called an ambulance. . . ."

"What hospital?" O'Moore demanded, and there was a sinking coldness in his heart. The clerk was staring at him curiously.

"The city hospital, I suppose, sir," he said slowly, "but I'm not sure, and. . . ."

"The phone call, man !" O'Moore threw at him. "If she called an ambulance, there must be a record of the call. I warn you that if anything has happened to Miss Martin, I'll hold you and your company strictly accountable !"

The man ducked down the hall to a doorway and O'Moore, just behind him, peered over his shoulder into a cubicle where a girl sat at a telephone switch-board.

"No, sir," she was saying. "There was no call from room forty-seven. I've been on duty all evening, and there hasn't been any at all. Miss Martin sent for a messenger, but she just asked me to phone for one. That's all !"

The clerk fluttered his hands. "I don't understand, sir," he said. "The ambulance men said Miss Martin had phoned them. There was a doctor and they went right upstairs. Miss Martin was almost unconscious, and. . . ."

O'Moore leaned toward the woman. "I don't suppose you remember what the doctor looked like?" he asked with a smile. "A handsome man, now?"

The girl smiled, patted her hair. "He had on dark glasses," she said. "I thought at the time it was kind of funny."

"Yes, indeed. Very amusing," chimed O'Moore. "Get me Mogul seven—three-eight-hundred."

He laid a coin on the switchboard beside her, was aware of the shivering of the clerk at his side. "Really, sir," he stammered. "Miss Martin called for the ambulance. We don't maintain surveillance on our guests. I'd be glad to show you her room. There is, perhaps, some message."

O'Moore smiled faintly. "Yes, and so you shall . . . show me her room," he murmured. "Ah, you have the call? Thank you, I'll take it right here ! Is that Flinn there? Good. O'Moore here. Moriarity Aloysius O'Moore. Are those gentlemen still in my chambers? Good. Then convey to Mr. Davis my compliments and request that he come to the Washington Hotel with all possible speed ! Tell him, he will find me here—and that the young lady he found in my apartment has quarters here ! Thank you, Flinn." He handed back the mouthpiece to the girl, and turned toward the clerk. "Mr. Davis," he said softly, "is a policeman ! Now, you may take me to Miss Martin's room. *Quickly !*"

THE clerk's eyes strained wide and he backed out of the phone room before he turned and scuttled along the hall. O'Moore noticed that the man held his right leg stiffly—and a mocking smile curved his lips. He kept the clerk before him as they stepped into the antiquated elevator and, afterward, while the cage creaked laboriously up the shaft. Now and then, the clerk shot a frightened side-glance toward him. He mumbled incessant apologies, pleaded for the "reputation of the house." O'Moore laughed sharply, and as the elevator creaked to a halt at the fourth floor, he thrust the man before him into the narrow, dim-lit hall.

O'Moore let his eyes sweep the corridor keenly. No light showed beneath the doors, and the number, *47*, gleamed on a door at the extreme end of the hall. The clerk's big ring of keys jingled in his shaking hand. He pressed the bull-push in the panel of *47* and the jangling of the bell within was loud. The emptiness of the gesture wiped the smile from O'Moore's lips, but he waited while the clerk turned the key, opened the door a slit.

"You serve your masters well," whispered O'Moore. "No, don't bother to pull that weapon out of your trouser leg! You'd never live to use it! *Ah, you would!*"

In spite of O'Moore's order, the man raked a knife out of his trouser leg, a long-bladed and vicious weapon. O'Moore's left fist flashed straight and hard to the jaw, and his right lifted in a flashing uppercut. The clerk's heels jerked clear of the floor and his shoulders were driven against the door. As it flew wide, O'Moore's hands shot out to seize the man's lapels, and he lifted him as a shield before him as he went into the dark-shadowed room. His shadow leaped before him, silhouetted by the slash of yellow light that reached in through the doorway—and then, inside the room, a woman screamed!

O'Moore saw her jerk bolt upright upon the bed, with the bedclothes caught to her breast. There was the crack of a gun, and powder-flame lanced toward him through the blackness! He felt the body of the clerk jerk in his hands from the impact of lead. Even as he flung forward with a cry of warning, he heard behind him the rush of many feet. They were soft-slippered, shuffling feet.

The yellow men were at his back!

CHAPTER FIVE

Into the Trap!

O'MOORE'S brain was stunned with the surprise of the thing that was happening. He had suspected treachery on the clerk's part, and yet his story of Aloha's kidnapping was convincing. The phone girl had corroborated it. But when he invaded Aloha's room, he was met with bullets and a scream—and Aloha was in bed!

The thing made no sense at all, and his shout that he was O'Moore did not stop the bullets. Two more thudded into the body of the clerk before O'Moore heaved it toward the bed, and leaped after it to wrench the gun from the girl's hand. Yet O'Moore felt jubilance bubbling through his veins at Aloha's safety.

"You little fool!" he cried gaily. "Is that the way to greet a guest?"

He was twisting toward the door as he spoke, one hand still braced against the bed.

Then two men spun into that narrow slash of light and the gun kicked against O'Moore's stiffened wrist. One man pitched forward across the threshold. The second staggered back with a hoarse cry and dodged past the opening. O'Moore reached the spot in a long bound, dragged the body clear, then slammed and locked the door.

He laughed as he groped for the light

switch, for it seemed to him that the battle was won. The police were on the way, since his keen eyes had spotted the treachery of the clerk in time. Aloha was safe and would clear him of the murder charge against her sister. He had the ruby securely hidden. He found the switch, flicked on the lights and swung toward the bed. Then a cry burst from his lips, and he squeezed off another shot!

The girl had climbed from her bed and was standing on the window sill prepared to jump!

O'Moore's bullet gouged the window frame beside her hand as he had intended, and the girl twisted about a terrified face —but it was not the face of Aloha! Dark eyes were narrow in a flattened sallow face, and her coal-black hair was wrapped in a coif about her skull. By all the gods, a Chinese!

O'Moore's lips pulled cold against his teeth. "Get down from that window," he ordered coldly, "or 'the next bullet will break your spine!"

The girl shuddered and got down slowly from the sill. Her night gown was sheer silk and it clung to the rounded litheness of her body. Her breasts lifted with quickened breathing, strained against the bodice.

"Please," she said uncertainly. "Please, I did not know it was a gentleman. I think. burglars!"

O'Moore was moving toward her, and his voice was light. "How could I question a lady's word?" he asked. "The police will come, of course, and the register will show you occupy this room. And, of course, you have a permit for this gun? I thought so. If a man forces his way into your room and you kill him, no one could blame you!"

The girl was moving toward him on narrow, naked feet. She looked up into his face. "I do not understand." she said hesitantly. "I have no wish to kill anyone!"

O'Moore smiled. "I'm sure you haven't," he said. "Permit me to return your gun!"

He polished it with a silken handkerchief and his ears kept keen watch on the hallway outside the door. There were men there, whispering together. In a moment, they would attack. He smiled, bowed as he handed the automatic, butt-first, to the girl!

Her hand struck like a snake, seized the gun. Instantly, she was squeezing the trigger, with the muzzle leveled for O'Moore's breast! But O'Moore laughed, for the gun only clicked emptily . . . and an instant later, he had taken it from her again. handling it carefully with the silken handkerchief.

"This," he said, "is the neatest trick of the week. The gun is registered in your name, as you say. Your fingerprints are on it now, and the bullets from this gun are in the clerk on the floor. And your little story won't save you, with him dead. for you see—*your bullets are in his back!*"

T HERE was no more pretense in the girl's face. Hatred glittered in her eyes, and O'Moore kept her carefully in sight while he sat at the desk and rapidly penned a note to the police which he fastened to the gun.

"This gun," he wrote, "murdered the clerk at the Washington Hotel. The fingerprints on it are those of the killer. and owner!"

He read that aloud as he wrote it while the girl glared at him unwinkingly. In the hallway, a gun blasted and a hole was punched in the door panel, but the bullet came nowhere near. He ignored it to keep his eyes on the girl.

"I'm sure you are beginning to get the picture, my Oriental lady," he said softly. "The police are on the way here. This gun goes into my pocket. Now, I don't want to be captured by the police, any more than I wish to meet your friends outside the door. It is up to you to see that I escape both."

"You lie!" the girl said sibilantly. "There are no police on the way!"

O'Moore smiled. From his pockets, he drew a large and intricately carved calabash pipe wrought in jade, and absently stuffed it with tobacco from a pouch of soft white leather. A heavy blow made the door shudder, and O'Moore glanced toward it with quick, wary eyes. It could not hold much longer. He was without his sword cane, because of the informality of his departure from the Mogul Club, and the gun in his pocket was empty. There was the knife which had fallen from the clerk's hand, but it was not a weapon to O'Moore's liking. He had the pipe lighted and he strolled toward the door, picked up a heavy chair and hefted it. Deliberately, he drove it against the wall so that a leg broke off. It had a brass claw foot, and it hefted nicely in his hand.

"Your friends will not take me," he told the girl. "And the police are on the way!"

As if to punctuate his sentence, a siren whimpered in the distance. When it wailed again, it was closer. Abruptly, the Chinese girl ran to his side.

"If I take you away from here," she asked quickly, "will you give me the gun?"

O'Moore laughed softly. "You were not meaning to accept my word? Of course not. Your quick mind has already devised a better method. You have a car nearby, for escape in case things went wrong. You will take me in that car, and then you will drive to a place where you will be sure to recover the gun. You will take me to the stronghold of your brothers in crime? That was your plan, was it not?"

The girl was backing away from O'Moore. He did not follow, but stood swinging the club gently against his leg, puffing blue clouds of smoke from his big pipe.

"It is a good plan," O'Moore said quietly. "If you will promise to do just that, I will go with you!"

A gleam of admiration touched the girl's impassive face. "You want me to deliver you into their hands, so that you can rescue the girl?" she said. "It is a good plan. I will help you!"

O'Moore's laughter boomed out. She would help him—to get a knife in his back!

He bowed to her, took the pipe from his mouth to gesture with it. "They lie who say there is no nobility in criminal hearts," he said. "I will testify to your great kindness. Lead on, Delilah!"

The girl ran lightly to the window, and once more mounted the sill. Outside the door, a man called out in a dialect O'Moore could not interpret, save that it was one of those barbarous run-together dialects of the high Himalayas. Before the girl could answer, O'Moore leaped to her side, and his eyes warned her to silence. She smiled at him.

"I help you!" she whispered.

SHE climbed to the sill then, and ducked under the sash. Men's shoulders surged against the door. Apparently, they had held back in hope that the girl would solve their problem for them. They had no way of knowing that O'Moore was unarmed, and his two swift shots had dropped two of their men. Now, guns blasted their lead through the panel, and it shuddered under a combined assault. It would not stand many more such blows!

But the Chinese girl was whispering. "That window below is open. Here is the rope!"

O'Moore grinned, "I'll go first, Delilah. It is only courtesy. . . . I have no doubts that you will follow me, as long as I have the gun. And I have no wish to have you prepare a trap for me below!"

As he finished speaking, he seized the rope and slid rapidly downward. The pipe was still locked in his teeth, the club thrust under his belt. For all his external ease, he was wracked with fears. The police were almost upon the hotel and after their entrance, he would have no chance at all. He thought that the girl he called Delilah would be forced to obey his orders, at least long enough to lead him into a trap ... but once inside the trap, what chance had he of emerging alive, much less of rescuing Aloha? O'Moore's jaw hardened to grimness. There was no other way!

He swung to the sill below, and Delilah was just behind him, sliding down the rope. He whipped through the window, but the room was empty. The girl's hand, catching his, was cold as some bloodless reptile, and he swung well behind her, kept a tight hold on that hand. He wanted no knife between his ribs!

A moment later, he was racing along the hallway behind the girl, and now he heard the sounds of flight overhead, the dying wail of the police siren. The yellow men were fleeing, at the approach of the law, and they must already have determined that he had escaped.

The way led through a cellar and up a flight of steps on a back street where a coupe was parked at the curb. Delilah slid in behind the wheel and O'Moore settled himself beside her.

"Before I walk into this trap of yours," he said placidly. "Go around to the front of the hotel ... and stop!"

The girl's head whipped toward him. Her careful braids of hair had become loosened and its black fringe swung across her shoulders. O'Moore leaned toward her.

"Either obey, or I will myself go to the police!" he said sharply. "And the gun goes with me!"

The girl muttered some sounds that were like curses, but the car leaped forward and, at O'Moore's sharp order, turned around the block toward the front

of the hotel, and the police. There was one white-topped police coupe in front of the hotel and, as they approached, another swept past O'Moore to skitter to the curb.

"Slowly!" O'Moore ordered.

He saw the broad-shouldered figure of Lieutenant Davis lurch from the coupe and, as the girl tooled the coupe past, O'Moore leaned his body from the window.

"Oh, I say, Davis!" he called.

The lieutenant whipped toward the sound of his voice and O'Moore waved a hand at him jauntily. "You remember me, what? Moriarity Aloysius O'Moore! Sorry, I can't stop and chat with you, old fellow, but I'm in something of a hurry, what?"

For an amazed instant while his mouth sagged and his eyes widened, Lieutenant Davis stared at the jauntily waving man in the window of the coupe. Then a hoarse shout broke from his lips. He clawed for his gun and began to bellow orders, darted back toward his car.

O'Moore settled into his seat beside the girl, tucked the pipe into his mouth again, and there was a satisfied smile on his lips.

"Now, Delilah," he said gently. "You may drive me into your trap. But I would advise you to go rapidly. Davis is anxious to talk to me. I might say he is frantic to talk to me. And I suspect that he will follow."

THE bellow of the coupe's motor almost drowned out the whine of the siren. He could depend on this girl doing her best to escape from the police; he did not think she would succeed, but neither did he think the police would overtake her swifter car! Meantime, Delilah would have little time to think up trickery ... and O'Moore would have help nearby when finally he entered the stronghold of the yellow men! So, he hoped. . . .

Of what would happen to him, to

Aloha, if the police over took him, he preferred not to think. He glanced at the pale intent face of the girl beside him as she drove the wide-open car, and he saw that the shoulder of her silken gown was torn. That was how he happened to see the reddened scar of an old burn on the flesh of her breast, and recognized it as a Chinese character. It was that recognition which brought a cry of horror to his lips!

He strangled it, but the girl shot a curious quick glance out of her eye corners and mockery glistened in them. O'Moore was gazing at her with a set grim smile.

"So," he whispered, "you are of the Bon of high Tibet, and of the Brotherhood of Amitabha!"

Delilah made no answer, but a slow smile curved her lips and there was cruelty in her face. She kept her eyes straight ahead. Black hair whipped about her head and she drove like a pale-faced demon. Already, the whine of the police siren behind them had grown fainter, but O'Moore scarcely was aware of that. Horror was gnawing at his heart with the thought of Aloha in the grip of the Brotherhood of Amitabha. Only once before had he seen the cabalistic brand of that vicious band, and he was not likely to forget the details. There had been another brave lad of Dublin who, like O'Moore, preferred the distant forbidden frontiers to the crowded cities of civilization. He had vanished into the highlands of Tibet, and when O'Moore had seen him again, he had such a brand on his chest.

Only there had been no recognition on the part of the man whom the police were carrying, strapped in a straitjacket, and bound rigidly to a stretcher. It would have been far kinder to kill him, but the British police were not allowed to execute madmen. They said that he never ceased to scream, as long as he lived; not even under the influence of opiates . . . No,

O'Moore was not likely to forget that symbol of the Brotherhood of Amitabha, the dreadful. Aloha was in the hands of these specialists in Oriental tortures! And they wanted information from her!

O'Moore grimly fought down the horror that was paralyzing his mind. Better, far better, to fall into the hands of police with the certainty of that unbeatable murder charge against him. But he could not allow himself that choice—for Aloha, brave Aloha with her dimpled smile, was their prisoner—and he knew of no way to save her except to throw himself into the trap toward which Delilah was speeding even now.

It came to him with a shock that he could scarcely hear the police sirens!

Even as the threat of that knowledge drove its way into his horror-numbed senses, Delilah threw the wheel over hard. The car scraped its metal in a dying scream against the brick wall of a narrow alley and Delilah turned toward him, as she brought the car to a halt.

"You asked to be driven into a trap," she said, and there was mockery in her tones. "I am glad to have obliged you, Moriarity O'Moore!"

O'Moore murmured, absently: "Pleasant of you, I am sure. I shall have to keep my word now, and return the automatic to you." His mind was racing feverishly. Somehow, he had to draw the police to this spot, and he knew that he had only seconds in which to work. In the rear vision mirror, he caught the flitting shadows of men as they closed in behind the car . . . so retreat was cut off.

With apparent absent - mindedness, O'Moore tapped the bowl of his pipe against the side of the car and spilled a deluge of sparks down upon the upholstery. Afterward, he took out his cigarette lighter to relight the pipe.

Delilah laughed, and called out in the strange dialect that O'Moore did not know. The men crowded forward instantly, and O'Moore just had time to thrust the cigarette lighter down beside the cushion before the door was whipped open and he stared into the leveled muzzle of an automatic.

The man grinned with an ironic display of teeth, yellow like a rat's. "Be pleased to descend, O'Moore *sahib*," he murmured. "The master, and another, wait for you!"

O'Moore nodded absently and stepped to the ground, heard with a cold sinking of his heart the police siren sweep by on the main thoroughfare and fade into the distance. He had been a fool to allow himself to be trapped like this. At the beginning, he had been sure he could draw the police to the spot. And if he failed he had counted on the bargaining power of the ruby, of which he alone knew the whereabouts. But that had been before he knew that he was dealing with the Brotherhood of Amitabha! They would not need to bargain—for they had ways of making men tell what they wished to know!

CHAPTER SIX

The Right to Laugh

BUT O'Moore's head was carried jauntily, and the pipe of jade was still clenched between his strong teeth. He sauntered between the hostile lines of Eurasians with their ready guns and their hating eyes, and he did not bother to glance toward them. He might have been a king for whom they had gathered to offer homage. They went in through an iron-sheathed doorway and he found himself in the service entrance of an office building. The main hallway was deserted, and O'Moore walked directly to the elevators.

"Good that I was expected," he murmured. "I do detest to be kept waiting."

There was no answer from the encircling men. Five of them stood well back from him with their guns ready in their fists. Delilah leaned carelessly against the wall. Her lack of attire, her bare feet seemed to bother her not at all. Her sprawling black hair, and the eager gleam of her black eyes turned her into something witch-like and fearful. O'Moore was straining his ears for some sound that would show the police had spotted the place. He had had time to make only hurried plans for summoning them, but the sparks he had dumped upon the seat of the coupe had been hotly burning, and the fuel from the upended cigarette lighter should help. In a few minutes, or longer if the upholstery must smolder for a while first, there should be a hot fire blazing in the coupe. The police would identify the license number . . . he hoped! If that failed, he must contrive something else.

The elevator sighed to a halt in the shaft, and the door was flung wide.

"Enter, O'Moore *sahib*," a voice hissed behind him.

The cage sped upward and the men with their guns were pressed close about O'Moore. He felt coldness crawling along his spine. He knew the politeness of the East, and what in this case it portended. These men would cut his throat with a murmured apology! He watched the floors slide downward past the elevator's entrance.

Thirty—thirty-five—forty. . . . It was at the fifty-fifth floor that the cage finally slid to a halt.

When the door opened, he was looking down a vista of ancient armor, of showcases in which metal glistened. He realized with a tightening of his eyes that he was in a museum of Oriental arms, and the thought of those weapons close to his hand stirred his hopes. Then all of that was wiped from his mind, for he was marched straight thought that corridor of weapons and through an arch to the left—and his heart lifted and thudded painfully against his ribs, and anger made the blood hum in his ears!

This chamber of the museum was fitted up entirely as an Oriental throne-room, and here the decorations were the torture machines at which the East was past master! For the moment, O'Moore scarcely was aware of that last fact. He was gazing straight at the throne, and the man who sat upon it, clad in all the fripperies of the East, cloth of gold and corruscating jewels. The sceptre in his hand was topped with a human skull! But the face of the man . . . It was Nachi! Behind the stiff-faced Eurasian on the throne the dread symbol of Amitabha had been drawn in blood upon a square of silver velvet.

He gazed straight at Nachi, because he dared not look at what was placed just to the left and before that throne. But the image of the thing he had seen there burned its hot way through his brain. It made his walking a stiff effort, and it turned his heart to a fire of rage. What stood there was a Chinese torture rack. and swinging in it, suspended by wires that were tied to tortured thumbs, legs festooned in weights that were dragging out her sweet life, was . . . Aloha! *

H ER head sagged forward so that her silken hair formed a veil before her ravaged face and most of her clothing had been torn from her body so that the cording strain of those hideous weights upon her feet showed terribly. The thin wires that bound her had cut deep . . . No, O'Moore dared not look lest he lose all reason and hurl himself blindly upon these fiends! No safety lay in that. He must keep his head and think, and think. Bitter and mocking laughter strangled on his lips.

"Greetings, O'Moore *sahib,*" murmured Nachi from the throne. "You have come in time to help us decide a nice problem. My friends here contend that it will take another fifty pounds upon the feet of our prisoner to shred her thumbs from her hands. I insist that they underestimate the tensile strength of human flesh, and that she can stand another hundred pounds at least. Certainly twenty-five will not do the job, as you shall see!"

One thin-boned hand lifted from the arm of the throne, and a slave glided forward with a weight in his hands. O'Moore forced himself to turn his head slowly toward where Aloha hung. The wire that linked her ankles already bore a half dozen such weights. As he stared with hot dry eyes, Aloha lifted her head with a slow and titanic effort so that for a moment, the hair parted its veil and she could look into his eyes. Muscles jerked in her shoulders, and her head wrenched back between her shoulders as the added weight was dropped into place.

"Oh, kill me!" she gasped. "Please, in God's name . . ."

Her head sagged forward and O'Moore knew with infinite relief that she had fainted. Something snapped in his hand, and he looked down slowly to see that the tightening of his fist had snapped a carved jade ornament from the base of his pipe. He stared at it stupidly through a long moment, then fumblingly he reached into his pocket and drew out a tobacco pouch, began to fill the pipe. He saw with a sense of unreality that his hands did not tremble.

"You Eastern pigs are all alike," he said deliberately. "Without imagination, even in such filthy work as torture. I beg of you, do not bore me with it. . . ." He had to stop then a moment, for the fierceness of anger closed his throat. "I beg of you, bore me no more with it! I came to talk business. I hear the brotherhood of Amitabha has lost a certain jewel!"

Nachi leaned forward and cruelly curved his thin lips, and O'Moore heard the thin hissing of the indrawn breaths of the men about him. Damn it, would the car never blaze forth its summons to the police! He couldn't stand here much longer while . . . while Aloha suffered! He knew, without looking, that the gunmen had moved closer to him!

"Your men searched my apartment, and did not find the ruby," O'Moore said with enforced quiet. "On the way up in the elevator, they searched my body, and they know I do not have it with me. I, and I alone, know where the ruby is . . . and so I will talk business with you. But only when you have ceased these amateur efforts at torture."

The smile on the leader's lips stretched until his teeth, discolored by opium, showed blackly between them. His voice came evenly, light with suppressed happiness. "We will be glad to allow you to experiment in torture, O'Moore *sahib*. That would give us pleasure, but concerning the jewel, the Eye of Rin-Po-Che, there can be no talk. You will surrender it at once! If you refuse, O'Moore *sahib*, we will demonstrate that we have other and more novel methods of torture. The girl first; yourself afterward, and. . . ."

There was the sharp clanging of the elevator door as it was flung open, and the loud voice of a white man lifted in anger. O'Moore felt his heart surge upward; and then sink in dismay. It was Lieutenant Davis who spoke, but it was not the voice of a man in command. It was the voice of a man, helpless in the hands of his enemies, and protesting only in futile rage!

O'MOORE knew then that he had failed in that effort also; and that there could be no rescue for Aloha and himself save for his own keen brain. And his mind would not work. It was dazed with horror, numbed by the torment of what was happening to Aloha. Davis was thrust roughly to his side, and the voices of the men who had brought him lifted in chattering explanation. Anger made the eyes of Nachi glisten and he swept them toward O'Moore with calculation.

"It was clever, O'Moore," he said flatly, "to set the car afire, but the stupidity of the police has saved us from serious annoyance. It was necessary to destroy this man's assistant."

O'Moore turned his head toward Davis, saw how anger reddened his square-cut face, and the savagery of his thin-set lips.

"Good evening, Lieutenant," he said gravely. "I don't suppose you have a match? I find my pipe has gone out on me."

Davis' head swung toward him and he spat out an oath—and then he saw the white, down-turned face of Aloha in the torture rack. Davis' own face turned grey and sick, and he struggled against the grip of his captors. O'Moore saw that all their attention was focused on Davis and he masked the sudden hope in his eyes by lowered lids. He fumbled in his vest pocket and took out a packet of matches.

"You don't mind, Nachi?" he asked.

Nachi's eyes swung toward him fiercely, and O'Moore let the pipe sag between his teeth so that its bowl was pointed toward Nachi. He closed his eyes tightly and touched a match gingerly to the bowl. A spurt of blazing white brilliance flared from the bowl of the pipe! There was a muffled blast that wrenched the pipe from between O'Moore's teeth, and frightened screams burst from the men about him. In the same instant, O'Moore sprang into action, like a sprinter at the crack of the starting gun!

A sideways leap took him beside the men who clung to Davis. Their hands were locked across their eyes, blinded by the glare, but O'Moore could see plainly. He wrested guns from their hands, and swung toward the throne . . . Nachi was gone! Even the throne had vanished in that split-second of darkness!

O'Moore cursed harshly, and swung toward the exit—and a solid phalanx of guards was charging toward him, guns in their fists! O'Moore threw lead toward them, and heard Davis fling himself violently into the battle. His curses lifted harshly, then his gun began to speak also. Four of the charging men were down, but the others stopped, took deliberate aim!

O'Moore's voice lifted clearly. "I wouldn't shoot, you chappies!" he called. "If you kill me, the ruby will be lost to you forever!"

Like an echo of his words, a magnified voice crashed out and O'Moore recognized that it was Nachi speaking through some sort of loud-speaker arrangement. Once more, it was in the dialect of the Himalayas. Before he had finished, the attackers had vanished backward through the archway!

"Cut down the girl!" O'Moore whispered to Davis. "This will last only a few seconds. There's a door behind her. I don't know where it leads, but it's the only way out! Neither she nor you is protected by the amnesty Nachi just ordered!"

Nachi's voice echoed in the room once more. "Fool!" he said. "Stupid pig of the West. What do you think to gain by this? You will only prolong your own suffering, and that of the girl. Throw down you guns, and surrender. I promise that for every second you keep me waiting, the girl shall suffer another hour!"

"Quickly," O'Moore whispered.

He heard Davis draw in a quick breath. "Okay!" the man muttered. "It's the first time I ever took orders from a woman-killer, but it seems to be your deal!"

O'Moore crouched behind the dais on which the throne had rested and tried to find the button or lever that he knew must have snapped Nachi down through the floor to safety. If he could just get hold of Nachi. . . .

"Already," came the purring voice of Nachi, "you have inflicted ten extra hours of torture upon the girl. Throw down

your guns, fool! Ten seconds more I will give you, and then my men come in. They shoot well. Their bullets do not have to *kill!*"

BESIDE him, O'Moore heard the thud of the weights on the floor as Davis released Aloha—and he could not find the hidden spring that would reveal Nachi's hiding place. He lifted his voice tauntingly.

"But my bullets always kill, Nachi!" he cried. "Many men will die before one can reach me with his lead . . . and even then I will keep on killing! I will still make a trade with you, Nachi. Our lives for the ruby!"

Davis' voice reached him hoarsely. "Come on, damn it!"

O'Moore straightened and threw a glance toward Davis. The lieutenant had Aloha in his arms and was moving toward the door. And in that moment, there was a rush of padded feet and guns began to blast! With a long leap, O'Moore placed his body between Davis and the girl and the killers. The two guns in his fists kicked in unison! Two men in the forefront of the new charge pitched to the floor and the rest flung themselves prone in the protection of those bodies, began to take deliberate aim! And O'Moore flung back his head and sent his booming laughter through the throne room of the Brotherhood of Amitabha!

"Come, yellow dogs!" he cried. "Come and meet your death at the hands of a man! Faith, it's the best fight that Moriarity Aloysius O'Moore has had in many a day!"

The guns kicked against his stiff wrists, braced against his hips. He sent a bullet burning across the neck of a dead man and through the head of a prone killer. The man beside him flinched, and so O'Moore spared him for a moment to pick off another who was taking more deliberate aim.

"Come on, fool!" Davis whispered behind him. "The door's open!"

O'Moore laughed and backed slowly toward the door. The barrels of his guns were restless as snake's heads, and as deadly. His lead flung everywhere and there were men writhing on the floor.

Nachi's voice raked out raspingly. "His guns are almost empty! Charge! But keep them alive. They deserve to die *slowly!*"

O'Moore flung his last bullets at the men as they ripped to their feet, then with a high taunting laugh, he whipped backward through the doorway and slammed the door shut.

"They won't come too fast," he cried, and his chest was still pumping with battle laughter. "Reload the guns while I barricade this door!"

He tossed his revolvers toward where Davis stood and palmed the wall to find the light switch. Behind him, Davis swore in a curious, thin voice, and O'Moore whipped about to stare toward him. Davis had the guns in his hand but his eyes were blankly on O'Moore.

"All my bullets are thirty-eights," he said slowly. "These guns are forty-fives!"

O'Moore swore, too, and his eyes swept about him—then the laughter of self-mockery swelled in his throat. For they were in a small store room, not more than ten feet square, and the door by which they had entered was its only exit save a window that looked out on fifty-five stories of empty space!

"Fools! Fools!" the voice of Nachi came clearly through the locked door. "Did you think to escape me? You are trapped, and your hours are numbered! Surrender now, lest the patience of Nachi become exhausted. Surrender, before the hours of your torture number more than the hairs of your heads! Once, a man lived for a month under the tortures of Amitabha! I think, in your case, you will survive even longer . . . and you shall discover that, even in such filthy business as torture, we have imagination!"

And Nachi laughed, hissingly, exultantly!

O'Moore drew in a slow breath and considered the door narrowly. It was strong, but it could not long endure the attack of the massed men outside. There was no hope that the police would hear shots so high in the air. He shook his head ruefully.

"I'm afraid," he said slowly, "that Nachi has won the right to laugh!"

CHAPTER SEVEN

The Axe Flashes

O'MOORE turned from the door, and the raucous taunts of Nachi's voice and moved toward where Davis had laid Aloha upon a dusty desk. He bent over the girl's white strained face. That tiny mole like a beauty mark was pitiful now, and he picked up her poor swollen hands and, sharply, snapped the dislocated thumbs back into their sockets. The pain wrung a moan from the girl, and her eyes opened. For an instant, she stared wildly about her, and then a faint smile moved her lips, and for a dim instant the dimple showed.

"I knew you'd come," she said simply, "but we didn't get away, did we?"

O'Moore grinned down at her, "Don't worry about it," he told her. "We will."

"Sure," rasped Davis. "We'll sprout wings and hop off from this window!"

He had opened the sash and was peering out into the darkness, his red hairy hands, pressed down on the sill, were whitened at the knuckles.

"If only I had some ammunition!" he groaned.

O'Moore was still smiling gently down into the girl's face, and her hands, painfully swollen, lifted to touch his arm. Her mouth twisted at the pain.

"Promise me," she whispered. "Promise me that, at the end, you will . . . will save me from the torture!"

O'Moore's grin grew stiff on his mouth, and he felt the rigidity creep coldly across his cheekbones. "I promise you," he said.

Then he whirled and his eyes, pale with desperation, skimmed over the things stored in the room. Besides the old desk, there was a suit of armor upon a rusted upright rod for display. His eyes narrowed on a bronze battle-axe leaning beside it. If it came to a finish fight . . . His eyes quested on impatiently. There was a rusted javelin leaning in a corner, some clothing in dust cloths hung upon a rack. That was all. O'Moore swore softly, and crossed to the window with long, quick strides. Nachi was still enjoying himself over the loud-speaker, but O'Moore scarcely heard the words. Davis stepped aside with a heavy, sardonic wave of a hand toward empty space, and O'Moore took his place.

Theirs was the highest building in the neighborhood and the upper windows of all the others were dark. Too far to reach the roof. Not even a hint of a ledge that they might walk. He peered downward and his lips twisted sardonically. There was not even another window below this one. Only blank wall stretched below. Davis had spoken truly. They would need wings!

O'Moore leaned farther out of the window and peered downward. The courtyard of the building was directly below, and there was a long walkway that ran straight out to a street that was empty of traffic. Across its dark shadowed width, there was a bank whose watchman's light burned dimly behind great plate-glass windows. O'Moore eyed that bank with narrowing eyes. If only there were some way of signalling the watchman, and summoning police . . . O'Moore strangled sardonic laughter. As well wish for wings!

He whirled back to the room and Davis was watching him gloomily. "I have to hand it to you, O'Moore," he said. "You certainly tied them in knots for a while. What the hell did you put in your pipe?"

"Flashlight powder," O'Moore said impatiently. "I put some in my tobacco pouch back at the apartment to use on you if the other trick failed."

Davis' face took on a ruddy glow of anger, and his dark eyes narrowed slightly, but he said nothing. O'Moore's eyes were questing once more over the room, and Nachi was shouting.

"The patience of Nachi is exhausted," he proclaimed. "Now, we will come after you! Break down the door!"

As an echo of his words, something heavy thudded against the solid door, and O'Moore nodded slightly. It would hold for a while; better if the heavy desk were rammed against it and held in that position, but he could not disturb Aloha. As if she read his thoughts, the girl pushed herself up from the desk.

"You'll need this," she said faintly.

SHE staggered on her swollen ankles and would have fallen but for O'Moore's quick arm. He carried her across the room and ripped down the rack of clothing for her to lie upon. Davis wheeled the desk across the room.

O'Moore gripped his fists hard against his thighs. Damn it, there had to be a way out of this! He couldn't let Aloha die now! His jaw shut tightly. Nevertheless, if he failed to find a way out, he would . . . would keep his promise to . . . spare her the torture! It was the least he could do.

Abruptly, O'Moore laughed. Davis wrenched about his head, and there was a sudden surprise in his eyes as if he had expected to find O'Moore gone raving mad.

"You're going to laugh yourself to death one of these days!" he said angrily. "What the hell there is to laugh about . . ."

But O'Moore was paying no attention to him at all. In a long bound, he caught up the javelin from where it stood in the corner and was weighing it in his hands. It was a heavy weapon with an iron point that was a third as long as the javelin itself.

He said, lightly, "If you were a watchman in a bank, Davis, and you heard a window crash in, what would you do?"

Davis looked at him with concentrated attention. "Call the cops, set the alarm ringing, and start shooting!"

O'Moore nodded. "Thereby showing admirable presence of mind, Davis," he grinned. "I see now why you're a lieutenant!"

Davis swore under his breath but held his eyes on O'Moore with the same strained attention. "Even if you could do that," he said, "the cops wouldn't have any way of knowing where the damned thing came from. They couldn't hear shots, even if we had anything to shoot. And those devils will be too smart to use guns now."

The hammering at the door was making the wood creak. A slight crack appeared in the upper panel. Over his shoulder, O'Moore flung an order at Davis. "Get the noses off those bullets of yours and make a heap of the powder. We might be able to work a flare. There may be time."

He poised the javelin in his hand, stepped carefully back from the window. His eyes were narrow, and the line of his jaw showed small bunches of muscle, but the smile lingered on his lips.

"I once killed an ounce with one of these gadgets," he said softly. "A snow leopard, you know. On the Amur in southern Siberia. Thing must have been seventy-five yards away. Natives started calling me 'mister' after that."

Davis made no answer. Aloha had braced herself up against the wall and she had drawn a scarlet cloak about her shoulders. O'Moore's eyes touched her briefly and she gave him her smile. His arm came back and he took a single stride—and hurled the javelin! At the same moment, there came a louder crash from the door, and the edge of an axe gleamed briefly before it was wrenched free again for another blow. O'Moore was leaning far out of the window, and his eyes were strained after the javelin. It arched far out into the night, but it was too soon to gauge where it would strike. The angle, from this terrific height, would be extremely narrow. If he missed the window, there would be no second chance. Behind him, the axe crashed again . . . and then a cry leapt to O'Moore's lips!

Faintly, through the darkness, there came the crashing clatter of breaking glass!

Davis swore violently. "Did it, by God!"

O'Moore whirled toward him, and saw that he had succeeded in getting the noses off only two bullets! His eyes pivoted toward the door, and he saw the barrel of a gun thrust through the widening crack! There would be no time for that flare!

"Will you surrender, fools?"

O'Moore reached the suit of armor in a long stride, picked it up bodily and staggered to the window. He balanced the headpiece against the glass.

"This is your last chance!"

O'MOORE bounded to where the battle axe leaned against the wall and whirled it overhead. Its keen edge was a nine-inch semi-circle of death and its ten-pound weight balanced like a flower in his powerful hand. O'Moore laughed softly at the feel of it.

"Come ahead, Nachi!" he called. "Come ahead—and die!"

For an instant after he spoke, there was silence and, faintly from the street, he caught the strident clamor of the bank alarm.

Aloha cried out joyfully, "Oh, the police will come now! We'll be saved!"

O'Moore threw a warning glance at Davis and caught the police lieutenant's slight answering nod. Davis understood well enough. Even if the police arrived before the yellow men beyond the door had made an end of them, there was slight chance that the men in the street would know anything of the battle being waged to the death high above their heads. If they discovered this, they still must climb to the fifty-fifth floor and wade through a swarm of yellow men. Meantime, O'Moore with his primitive weapon must hold back a score of men with modern arms! No, their chances of survival were not conspicuous!

DAVIS crossed to the suit of armor against the window, dragged out a sword fastened to the belt, one of the curved excellent blades of the East.

"Never used one of these things," he said gruffly. "But I guess I can after a fashion. O'Moore, in spite of what you did, you're all man!"

O'Moore grinned his answer, twirled the battle-axe. "These toys," he said, "are estimated to have killed more men than any other weapon in the world's history. I'll try not to diminish it's murderous reputation. . . . *Nachi, what's delaying you?*"

A terrific crash against the door answered him. The top hinge burst loose with an explosion like dynamite. The desk skated backward under the assault. O'Moore flicked off the lights of the tiny room.

He whirled the axe high above his head and leaped to the attack. His laughter was a war-cry. . . .

The heavy door lay like a ramp from threshold to desk, and there was a close huddle of the yellow men in the opening, hands still hard upon the long table they had used as a battering ram. The light

was behind them, and it put their faces in deep shadow from which their wide-straining eyes glistened furtively. These things O'Moore saw in a single swift glance. His charging leap carried him to the ramp of the fallen door and he sprang through the doorway and was in the midst of the men before they could recover their balance.

Only one man was ready for that attack. He stood just back of the others with an automatic in his fist, and the axe reached for him in a sweeping down-arc. He saw it coming and his mouth split in a scream. His left arm flew up futilely as a ward for his head! But that axe had been made for biting through steel armor. It pinned the arm against the man's head and lopped it off like a stick of kindling, and it passed on to bite deep into the chopping block which was the man's skull.

In the act of striking, O'Moore shortened the blow so that it was the outer slicing lip of the axe-edge that bit and the continuation of the stroke swept it free even when it bit deepest. O'Moore shouted and swung the axe in a sideways circle toward his left. It glanced across the head of the first man and drove him hard down on his face. His feet flew up. That murderous blade caught the second man just below the jaw, and checked briefly there. But the third man, and the one nearest the door sagged to his knees beneath the continuation of that stroke. There was a twisted grimace of hatred on his face as it swung toward the light and his clawed hand was sweeping a gun upward. Above his head the axe hissed and its edge bit deep into the frame-work of wood!

O'Moore shouted and drove his heel into the man's uplooking face, then leaped backward through the doorway with the haft of the axe in his fists. It tore loose from its bite in the wood and O'Moore leaped to the floor inside the room. He saw Davis reach through the doorway with a chopping blow of the sword, and the man he had kicked straightened, kicking and screaming, upon the floor.

CHAPTER EIGHT

Death Is Welcome!

O'MOORE'S breath was coming quickly. The space before the door was clear for the moment, but he knew that the killers flanked it to either side. He could not make such another foray, but it had gained them a breathing space.

"Draw the sword a little toward you as it strikes," he called softly to Davis. "Use your wrist as a pivot as you would if you wanted to drive in a man's skull!"

Davis grunted. "So that's the trick of it. I was just thinking a night-stick would serve as well, though it did bite some."

From the darkness, Aloha whispered, "I hear police sirens!"

O'Moore listened with a strained attention, but the siren was very faint. It wasn't time yet to attempt a signal. "When I call out to you presently, my darling!" he answered Aloha, "come to this light switch and begin to flick the lights off and on. Three short flashes; three long flashes; three short ones again. It's just possible that someone understands an S O S, and . . ."

His voice broke off, for there was a slippered rush of feet, and a man leaped up the ramp of the door, and there were others swift on his heels! Davis' sword caught a glint of light as it swept sideways across the man's body, and the yellow man doubled over the blade with a soaring scream. O'Moore leaped close to the wall and swung his axe straight overhead while Davis fought to get his sword clear. O'Moore swore softly under his breath, for he saw that no one of these men carried a gun. Nachi had been too clever to permit one of them to bring with him a weapon that his prey might use! He struck again, and from close against the wall, a gun blasted its fiery spear of death into the room. The lead whispered intimately in his ear . . . and the axe struck

again! Too late, he saw the trick. His blade bit where a moment before the hand had been, wedged into the hard wood of the frame—and instantly, there was a swift rush of the killers!

O'Moore shouted a warning to Davis, heard his answering cry and saw the sword whirl to the attack. A good swordsman would never have struck like that. Davis put too much into each blow, and his recovery was too slow—and O'Moore's axe was still wedged tight in the wood. No chance now to wrest it free! With a harsh shout, O'Moore leaped forward!

His fist lashed against the jaw of the first and the man's back arched under the pile-driver force of the blow. He hammered back against the man behind him, but there were too many of them to be stopped by that trick. The pressure of the attack carried the unconscious man forward and O'Moore struck and struck again. He felt steel eat hotly into his thigh and, despite all he and Davis could do, he was being driven backward! Fury swirled into his throat, and he leaped to the floor, caught the feet of the first man in the ranks, and jumped backward. Even as he moved, he was twisting with a powerful heave of his shoulders. The yellow man screamed as his body began to whirl through the air. Once, and twice O'Moore performed his whirl with spurning feet, like a hammer-thrower in his ring. At each whirl he uttered a hoarse shout and at the third, he released the man!

It was a tremendous throw. Like a missile from a catapult, head-first, the man was hurled toward the door. The screaming wail from his lips raised thinly, and then his head struck the first of the killers and the sound broke off. Like a stand of ten-pins, the men went down before that battering ram. Only one of them, a long knife in his hand, ducked past and leaped straight at O'Moore where he reeled, off-balance, from the throw!

O'Moore saw the man coming, saw the

high sheen of the knife as it slashed toward his throat. He reached for the man's body, and went backward under the impact. But even in that moment of deadly peril, his mind worked swiftly. As he pitched backward to the floor, his feet lifted and drove hard into the man's belly ... and he timed his throw beautifully!

STRAIGHT over his head, the knife-man sailed. His scream blended with the dying wail of police sirens in the street below. Then there was a crazy mingled clatter of steel and breaking glass ... and afterward the scream lifted higher, and was in the air outside. O'Moore had thrown the man through the window, carrying the suit of armor and the window-frame with him! He staggered to his feet and the scream was still sounding, thinly now, faintly now, as the killer plunged toward the pavement fifty-five stories below! The scream cut off, and afterward there was the heavy tinny clatter of the armor striking the pavement, as if a kitchen full of pans had been dumped out of the window.

"It's a good trick if it works," O'Moore panted. "Aloha, start flashing the lights. Davis! Up with the door!"

A leap carried him to the door and Davis' powerful shoulder was suddenly beside his. The door slapped back into its socket, the desk wedged it in place—and from beyond, guns began to speak. Sparks of light stabbed through the wood where the bullets had ploughed, and Davis hurled himself against O'Moore, bore him to the floor.

Davis scrambled to his feet, dragged O'Moore aside. "You fool," he grumbled. "You crazy damned fighting fool!"

O'Moore had a smile on his lips, but there was strain in it. His head was swimming, and he could feel the strength flowing out of him with the warm rush of blood along his thigh—and his axe was gone! He pushed himself up from the

floor. The flicker of the lights was more blinding than darkness, and he could get only glimpses of the wound in his thigh; was aware of Aloha's face, pale above the scarlet and gold of the robe she had donned, and of her dark eyes turned toward him.

"You promised me," she cried. "If everything else fails ..."

O'Moore bent stubbornly over the wound in his thigh, ripped at his shirt to make a bandage.

He straightened when the bandage was hard about his thigh. "In the olden days of Ireland," he said softly to Davis, "they had a custom that was a grand and foolish thing. When the battle was lost, when the castle was hopelessly besieged and there was no choice between starvation and surrender, they made a sally. Not like the charge of cavalry. No, one man at a time. He walked out of the gate, and he circled the walls of the castle and, presently, if he lived, he cut his way back to that same gate again. It was a more honorable form of harakiri."

From beside the lights, Aloha cried out faintly. "No! You promised!"

O'Moore took the sword from Davis' hand. "It will gain us a little time," he said. "If it does not gain enough, you will know your duty to Aloha."

There was a swift, stumbling rush of feet and Aloha was in his arms, close against his chest in the darkness. "No, dear," she said. "See, the door is holding them. There is no need!"

There was a crash on the door, then, and a slow heave, and a slice of light appeared on the ceiling and widened. O'Moore put Aloha gently from him.

Davis said, sharply, "The sword is mine!"

O'MOORE answered either of them. He sprang where the door was thrusting wide in the frame and the bright steel slashed through the crack. A blast of gunfire answered, and O'Moore reeled back from the searing breath of powder flame. And the door fell flat in a crashing thunder upon the floor. Behind him, he heard Aloha cry out frantically, and Davis' sharp curse . . . and then O'Moore made his sally! He made it with hard, taunting laughter on his lips and with the curved, long sword of a samurai in his fist—and men gave ground before the attack.

O'Moore's right leg was dragging from the wound, and still the men circled him. They had guns in their hands, but they did not use them. A thrown knife hissed past his ear as he dodged painfully. . . . And O'Moore laughed and leaped toward the killers.

Suddenly, Nachi's voice rang through the hall. "Shoot his legs out from under him, you fools! The police are in the street!"

O'Moore whirled toward the sound of the voice and saw the yellow, taunting face of Nachi in the broad arch at the room's end; saw the gun ready in his fist. And O'Moore shouted and began to run toward him.

Flame spurted from the gun in Nachi's hand, and O'Moore felt the shock of the lead. He faltered . . . and ran on! Another gun-flash. But if the lead struck him this time, he did not even feel it. Death was in his eyes, and in the dripping blade in his hand, and the strong, deep laughter of a fighting man was on his lips. He knew that if he could reach and kill Nachi, Davis and Aloha would be safe. The others might cut him down, but with the threat of police in the street, they would not have the courage to continue the fight afterward. Not if Nachi were dead!

O'Moore sobbed, with his laughter, and this time he felt the stroke of lead. Good God, he was on his knees! Behind him was the swift rush of slippered feet, and Nachi's voice was strong in triumph! O'Moore swore tearingly, and he picked up his fainting body and set it on his feet. The sword was a crutch in his hand, and there was death all about him. He braced his feet and swung the sword, and there were screams about him—and a sudden wide space in which were no men at all. But Nachi stood before him, the smile gone from his mouth, and fear glistening in his eyes.

Nachi steadied the gun across a forearm, and the muzzle was leveled at O'Moore's heart. And O'Moore, standing on braced legs, that shook beneath him, knew that he could never reach the man, knew that his strength was failing him as the breath drew it from his body. With a final bitter call upon his will. O'Moore whipped back his sword arm and sent the blade whistling through the air toward that mocking yellow face. Flame leaped out to kick him in the face and, stiffly, as a centuries-old king of the forests falls, O'Moore pitched forward on his face.

PAIN brought O'Moore back to his senses and he knew the fearful sinking coldness of failure. But, what of the girl? What of Aloha? Had Davis kept his promise, and . . . O'Moore stirred uneasily, and he found that his arms could lift. He opened his eyes, and Aloha's face floated over him. Behind her was another blur that presently became the grinning hard-lined face of Lieutenant Davis.

O'Moore tried to struggle to his feet and found that he could only heave his body to a sitting position with great effort. He peered about him and saw the carnage his sword had wrought. And he saw the sword . . . and laughed. For his last desperate throw had been pretty good! The point had caught Nachi's face squarely in the middle, and it still jutted up stiffly above the supine Master of Amitabha, like a mocking steel tongue.

"Look here, Davis," O'Moore growled.

"you ought to know by now that I didn't kill that girl in my room. It was these beggars after the ruby. . . ."

Aloha's face was drawn with pain. "Yes, he believes that now," she whispered. "I explained to him. And I do not care if I never, never see that hateful ruby again. We were at school in Italy, and they would not let us take our money out of the country. It was all there, so we bought that ruby from Nachi . . . and he followed us to get it back. He was a false priest, and his life depended on recovering the stone.

"And, oh my dear, can you ever forgive me for sending that dreadful stone to you? I ran from you so that your life would not be in danger and then, when I reached my hotel, I realized that I had been drugged. It must have happened there in the night club. Before I succumbed to the drug, I sent the ruby to you."

Davis came forward gruffly. "I've known a lot of smuggler's tricks for hiding jewels, and we didn't find it in your apartment. You didn't have it on you when Nachi searched you."

O'Moore grinned. "If I can make it to the first floor," he said slowly.

He made it, with the help of Davis' shoulders beneath one arm, and Aloha's beneath the other. But it was a tender hand he laid upon her arm, when he stood once more on the first floor of the building.

"There is a certain magic necessary," he said, and the grin came back to his mouth. "It was the magic got me into this business in the first place, and I do not think without it, I can recall this ruby."

Davis was frowning impatiently, but a slow flush colored Aloha's cheeks.

"If you're sure it's necessary," she whispered. "But remember the trouble it got you into."

O'Moore sighed. "Faith, it's a trouble I'll be in all the rest of my life!" he said.

And Aloha put her arms about his neck and kissed him and O'Moore afterward said certain magic words that sounded suspiciously like, "I'm afraid, my dear, that such magic never ends!"

Davis said, grinning. "Did I hear something about a ruby?"

O'Moore grinned back at him and stooped over the jar of white sand beside the elevator doors and picked up a black mass of dottle that once, not so long ago, he had knocked from his pipe. He began to brush the fragments aside and, from its heart, there came a gleam like fire!

Davis swore harshly and O'Moore handed the ruby back to Aloha with a bow, but Aloha took it very carelessly and her eyes were on the laughing blue eyes of O'Moore.

"You know," she said softly. "I've always thought Moriarity was a beautiful name."

THE END

Into the night-shrouded swamp went Walter Parton, seeking the girl who long since had told him she was not fit to receive his love. Behind him sounded the shrill, devil-piping of that grinning god of hell, summoning his gold-horned beasts. And in his ears echoed the ghastly screams of Rose Loran from that hidden hut of evil where, people whispered, the marks of cloven hoofs had put Satan's signature!

GIRL OF THE GOAT=GOD

NOVELETTE OF WEIRD, MYSTERIOUS DOOM

OUT OF the night a scream rose, high and thin and quivering. For a long minute it held, a scarlet thread of sound. Then it ended, and there was nothing but the rustle of breeze-stirred foliage and the shrill grating of the crickets, screeching an obbligato to terror.

Rose Loran was icily motionless, staring across vague lamplight at the black oblong of the window through which the shriek had come. In her cold hands the dishes she had just removed from the cluttered supper table rattled tinily, shivering with the uncontrollable tremble of

by Arthur Leo Zagat
(Author of
"Death Lands a Cargo," etc.)

her slight frame. A precariously balanced tumbler jittered against the edge of the tray, toppled, smashed to the floor. The kitchen door behind the girl crashed open.

"What was it?" Aunt Faith chattered.

"Rose! Where—I thought you. . . ."

Rose twisted, the older woman's gibbering fright paradoxically restoring control over muscles momentarily paralyzed by the horror of that scream. Faith Loran, tall and spare, her drawn, thin face ash-colored and twitching, clung to the door-jamb. Her grey, tired eyes were wide-pupilled, staring, and her gaunt neck was corded with fear.

"I—I don't know." The words rasped Rose's parched throat. "Someone in the garden. Someone—it—it didn't sound like anything human."

"The—the garden." The woman's pallid lips parted only slightly to let out the whispered syllables. "Elmer. . . . I sent Elmer . . . to the well."

"Oh Aunt Faith!" The exclamation was sharply rebuking. "In the dark! When you know he can hardly see in bright sunlight!"

But there was relief in Rose's voice, too. Now she understood that scream. The decrepit old man who was their one servant had stumbled, fallen hard, and screamed. That was all it was. There was no reason for this fear that tore at her, that squeezed her pounding heart. Rose turned, snatched up the lamp from the table, started for the great arched opening at the other end of the high-ceilinged, huge dining hall.

"Rose!" Aunt Faith's bony fingers clutched her biceps, digging in with convulsive strength. "Rose! Where are you going?"

"Out to Elmer. He's hurt. I've got to. . . ."

"No!" It was a tenuous, almost voiceless gust of sound. "Don't go out there! Don't go out there—in the dark."

"The dark!" Rose jerked away, exasperatedly. "I'm not a child. I'm not afraid of the dark."

She was, though. She was eerily terrified by the moonless murk out there. Aunt Faith had made her afraid of it, in the past few weeks. The way her aunt had insisted on locking all the doors and windows at nightfall; the way she would stand for hours staring out into the sightless gloom—these things had their effect

on the girl's nerves. She began to believe that her aunt expected to see something —dreadful. . . .

Only yesterday Rose had told Walter about Faith's queer behavior. Big shouldered, stalwart Walter Parton, the man who loved her and whom she loved. He had laughed, and then suddenly a tender fierceness had masked his broad-planed face. "Why don't you let me take you away from all this, Rose?" he had growled. "From this rotting house and this half-crazy aunt of yours."

"I can't, Walter," the girl had sobbed. "Why do you keep coming back and asking me? You know I can't marry you. You know I can't marry anyone. I daren't."

"I'll keep coming back, and I'll keep asking you till you say yes." How she had wanted to snuggle into those great arms of his, to feel his lips on hers! But she had pulled away and had told him to go, and he had climbed into his roadster and driven it away at reckless speed toward his home in Loranton. And she had gone slowly back to the shadows of Loran Hall and to the dread that had settled down upon it. . . .

THE dim gleam of her lamp could not fill the vast expanse of the entrance foyer. It slid over the lower steps of a baronial staircase, along papered walls whose intricate patterns were faded and drab, stopped at the patinaed, dark oak of a towering door. Rose went to the portal, tugged at its heavy bolt.

Aunt Faith was alongside her, was plucking fearfully at her sleeve. "Don't open it. For God's sake don't open it."

The girl thrust her shoulder against the aged spinster, shoved her away. "Please, Aunt Faith. You're hysterical. Elmer. . . ." The bolt came out of its socket, and the heavy door creaked slowly inward to her pull. The lamp-flame flickered, sent a filament of black smoke curling upward, then burned steadily in the lifeless air. A rotted board in the floor of the broad porch sagged under Rose's slight weight. The roof-high pilasters fronting the house were a row of pallid, gigantic spectres marching away on either side into obscurity. A peculiar, hushed oppression closed in on her, and the pungent aroma of lush greenery was in her nostrils, tainted with the miasmic breath of Gorham's Swamp that held the Loran Estate within the crescent sweep of its putrescent bog.

Rose hesitated, listening tautly. The night walled in the sphere of her feeble light, and repitilian tendrils of uncared for vegetation crawled over the verandah edge. A sound bubbled up through the sibilant sea of rural silence, a burbling, liquid moan. The girl's head jerked to it and it came again.

"Elmer! Where are you, Elmer?" Thick-clustered, rank foliage took her cry, swallowed it. Brambles tore at her dress as she ran down the thudding path, rosebush thorns sliced the skin of her bare arms. Rose stopped suddenly, her heart pounding.

Ahead something entered the rim of light, something that was moving. Something that writhed, agonizingly, and then was still.

."Elmer!" Rose could only whisper the name as dread clutched at her larynx. She drove herself a hesitant step forward —and then her feet went out from under her, sliding in the slippery mud. She rolled, got to her knees.

The lamp, jarred from her hand, had miraculously landed upright in the muck. Its light painted Elmer Stone's wrinkled face, twisted and almost unrecognizable. His face was drawn into lines of agony. His chest was a weltering horror of ripped overall cloth purplish with viscid, glutinous blood that spilled out of a deep

and horrible gash torn raggedly through his breast. The memory of a bull-gored farmer she had seen once, years ago, came to Rose's fainting mind. This jagged wound was like that. But there was no bull inside the high iron fence Faith had insisted on erecting around the place, and whose tall gate she made a ceremonial of locking at dusk. There was no animal of any kind. . . . What then, could have done this?

A bubbling moan pulled her staring gaze back to the tortured countenance. Elmer's eyelids were blue, ghastly membranes drawn tight over the bulging round of his old eyes. His seamed skin was wax-pale with the filming of death. But his blue lips twisted and words came bubbling out.

Rose bent closer, shuddering. Meaningless sounds came out of writhing agony. "Goat goatem . . . ." Meaningless sounds that suddenly were drowned by a spew of blood. The racked body arced with a spasm of uttermost anguish, flung over in its final, terrible convulsion. A lax arm flopped down in the mud and lay still. Elmer Stone didn't move any more. Rose knew that he would never move again.

"THE goat—the goat man," a wire-edged voice screamed over Rose's head and splintered into high-pitched laughter, into a cacchination utterly mad. *"The piper has come for his pay."*

The girl surged to her feet, swung about to face her aunt. Faith Loran's head was thrown back. The crazed laugh shrieked from her wide-open, contorted mouth. One thin, satin-sleeved arm was thrust stiffly out in front of her and a bony forefinger pointed rigidly—not at the shattered corpse but at something beyond. Rose whirled and saw a pallid, grotesque specter the lamplight just reached.

Panic struck at Rose for a frantic,

ghastly moment, and then she knew what it was at which the spinstress pointed. A statue of Pan the wood-god, haunched on shaggy goat legs, reed pipes at his saturninely grinning mouth. Curving horns jutted out of the touselled disorder of the carved hair. *Horns.* Good God! Was the stain darkening one of them only moss or. . . .

"The night—," Faith screeched between peals of crazed laughter— "The night of the Lorans. . . only us left to pay the piper. We who did not dance must pay him. . . . The sins of the fathers—"

Rose couldn't see the stone pedestal on which Pan squatted, but she knew what Aunt Faith meant. There was a rhyme graven into it, a lilting rhyme from over whose deep, angular letters a boyish Walter Parton had once scraped green slime so that they could read:

Dance ye mornyng, dance ye noon,
Dance ye sunlit hours away.
Length'nyng shadowes tell that
    soone
I will come to ask my paye.

The old woman's screaming laugh tore at Rose's nerves. It was harder to bear than even the sight of the mutilated corpse at her feet.

The Lorans had danced. God knew they had danced! Roy Loran the second had brought to the paradise, the first Roy had carved out of wilderness, carousing young bloods and complaisant ladies from the distant city. Roy the third, Faith's father and Rose's grandsire, had added new and terrible vices to the orgies of Loran Hall. He had died raving, calling down curses on the fourth Roy, who had killed Rose's parents in a drunken, wild auto ride and disappeared into the unknown.

"The bill is overdue and we must pay—" Pan seemed to be listening to Faith Loran's wild cries with his cocked head. He seemed amused, with cruel lines around his mouth belying his grin, with evil puckering his tiny eyes. . . . Suddenly Rose felt that she was going as mad as Faith.

"Stop it," she screamed. "Stop it." Her hand struck out and its palm slapped stingingly across her aunt's sere cheek. "Stop it."

The shrill laugh cut off, something like reason returned to the woman's staring eyes. She touched the red blotch left on her cheek by the girl's blow. "What happened to him?" she said haltingly. "Oh Rose. What could have done it?"

The girl shuddered. "Gored," she whispered. "A bull. . . ."

Faith shook her head. "No bulls anywhere near. And the gate is locked. Look." She clawed at her breast, pulled out a black ribbon through the seam of her blouse. A twisted, archaic key hung at its end. "I locked it and the only key has been with me all the time."

"But—what then . . .?" Rose shuddered, made herself look down again at Elmer. At the ground around the tragic heap drenched by water spilled from the bucket he had been carrying, by water and by. . . .

She was staring, staring unbelieving at the trampled mire. At black mud trampled and churned by feet whose imprints were glaringly, starkly plain in the light of the lamp set down among them. At sharply defined indentations that were filling with a slow seep of red-tinted moisture.

They were unmistakable. They were prints of cloven hooves. Of hooves too small to be a bull's or a cow's. They might have been made by goat feet . . . . .

A liquid ripple of shrill melody skirled out of the darkness, clotting the girl's thoughts. It changed to laughter—a sound of shrill, mocking glee. Such weird laughter as Pan's pipes might make if Pan were laughing into them.

Something darted across the light—a small stone smashing into the lamp. Its chimney crashed and darkness blotted out the scene.

"The goat man," Faith screamed. "Oh God. . . ."

A vast, formless bulk surged out of the darkness! Rose whirled, leaped into a frantic, desperate run. She sped up the path on the wings of fear. She ran endlessly through dank blackness filled with the stinging whiplash of unpruned branches, with the tripping tangle of untended vines. A hoarse breath panted behind her, and the thud, thud of ponderous, pursuing feet. Always behind her, and closer, closer. . . .

The house loomed ahead, its façade vaguely luminous. Across its porch Faith's vague form flitted, wild arms flailing above her head. She vanished into the gaping black maw of the open portal, and suddenly the dark oblong was narrowing, narrowing . . . .

"Don't," Rose screamed. "Don't close it. Don't close the door on me!" Her frantic feet pounded on wood, the single shallow step to the verandah, and something twitched at her dress from behind. A savage, bestial howl roared in her ears. A chattering howl of triumph.

CHAPTER TWO

Living Nightmare

THE feral roar goaded the frantic girl to a frenzied leap. It carried her across the porch and through a narrow opening left by the closing door. Metal, the rusted lockbolt, gashed her arm, but she squeezed through. She sprawled, breathless, and heard the dull thud of the shutting door, the rattle of its bolt, the pound of a heavy body against it. *A sound like rock pounding against the wood.* The house shook to the impact, but the great door held.

"The window," Faith screamed. "The window in the dining hall. The shutter."

Rose jerked around, staggered to her feet. She dived through blackness into the great room where they ate, flung herself across the floor to the open window. Her hand clawed for the handle of the iron shutter that had been put there for protection against Indian attack when the hall was built. She pulled at it, tugged it down. Feet pounded outside, and a face glared in at her. Small eyes glittered malevolently under a leathery low forehead. She glimpsed wide-nostrilled, swarthy features, a pointed, straggly beard, and then the clanging metal cut them off from her vision.

Rose pushed the hooked fastening home, reeled, clutching the sill to keep from falling. She pulled great sobbing breaths into her tortured lungs, and fought nausea twisting her stomach, fought madness swirling within her skull. Mad! She must be mad! For she had thought horns had projected from the brow of that evil countenance. She had thought it the visage of Pan, come alive.

Pan, alive and malevolent! It was her nightmare suddenly become real, the nightmare from which time and again had driven her into shrieking wakefulness, and left her trembling in her bed.

When she had been a lonely little child in this great house with only those two for company—her granite-faced grandfather with the agonies of hell smouldering in his eyes, and her dour-visaged aunt —she had used to pretend the sculptured godlet was a rollicking playmate, her own 'boy-friend.' When Walter Parton had come to play with her, there had been the three of them. Then had come the grandfather's last, terrible night, his shouted obscenities booming through the hollow emptiness of Loran Hall, booming through the locked door behind which she had cringed, shaken and terrified.

After it was over, after the old man had shouted his last curse and his profane lips were forever sealed, Aunt Faith had come to the cowering, white-faced fifteen-year-old. Trembling, distressed, she had told the girl the wild history of her ancestors.

The founder of the line had come here from the sea. He had purchased the good land from one Stannard Gorham for a song, leaving Gorham only the useless swamp. He had brought workmen from far away Providence to erect this mansion. When it was finished he had married a girl twenty years his junior. She had died giving birth to his son.

As if in defiance of Fate the first Loran had lavished all the luxuries the time afforded on his heir. There had been money to buy them with, gold money and silver from some mysterious, apparently inexhaustible store. Coins of alien mintage, some green and worn, some brightly new. The men who had built Loran Hall settled on Roy Loran's land. Loranton became a thriving community. Stannard Gorham repented of his bargain, came demanding restitution. He crawled away, after a while, broken in body and mind by that which had been done to him.

The inevitable had happened. Rose's great-grandfather had grown up a waster and a profligate. His son, the man whom Death had just claimed, had outdone him. And *his* oldest son had attained the apex of evil—and brought the house crashing down. The last that had been heard of the fourth Roy Loran, of Rose's Uncle Roy, was a report of his death in a speakeasy brawl on New York's Bowery. Grandfather had refused to claim the body.

"He said Potter's Field was too good for him," Faith had finished. "And that is the way the Loran line ended. We are

all that are left and the Loran heritage must die with us. Love and children are not for us."

It had dawned on Rose why Faith had never married. "Oh," she had sobbed. "Let's go away from here. Let's go away from this awful place."

"We can't," the woman had replied. "My poor darling, we can't. Grandfather has willed the Hall to us and what's left of the estate. But that is all there is. There isn't any money left. Those who went before us have danced, and we must pay the piper."

It was then that Rose understood why Stannard Gorham had astonishingly appeared during the festivities of the second Roy's marriage and presented the statue of Pan as a peace-offering. A peace-offering! He had mockingly placed his threat and his curse on the very lawn of his enemy. It was his hand that had graven that verse:

Dance ye mornyng, dance ye noon,
Dance ye sunlit hours away.
Length'nyng shadowes tell that
* soone*
I will come to ask my paye.

And when she had at last sobbed herself to exhausted sleep the dream had first terrified her. . . . The smell of goat-flesh in blackness. . . . A leering, lustful face close above her own—a man-face that was also the bearded and horned visage of a goat. . . . Calloused, irresistible hands gripping her shoulders, forcing her down. A hairy, repulsive hide pressed against her skin, flaying her with its shaggy roughness. . . .

The next day Rose, white-faced, her eyes downcast, a slime of evil seeming to her to foul her slender body, had sent Walter away. He had returned again and again through the three long years, and again and again she had dismissed him.

Each time she had fled to her room, weeping, reviling the fate that denied love to her. . . .

A FUMBLING rasp along the edge of the shutter at which she stared seemed to scrape the raw edges of her throbbing nerves. The corrugated metal bent inward a bit. Rose glanced frantically around the room, searching for some weapon, for anything that might serve to put up a futile battle against the dread thing that sought entrance. There was nothing. . . .

Dull pound of ponderous footfalls pulled her gaze back to the window. They faded. Had the killer, the—goat man—given up? Was he baffled by the defences Aunt Faith's senile mania had erected against him? *Against him!* She had known, then, that he was coming! *How had she known?*

He was not gone! Rose whirled to the sound of his probing fingers at the chamber's other window. He was making a circuit of the house. He was searching for a way in. . . .

The archway to the foyer filled with light, and then Faith was standing in it. From somewhere she had drawn courage, and she was again prim, stiffly erect in lustrous black satin, a high-boned collar jabbing into the parchment dryness of her skin, grey hair pulled tightly back from a brow whose fine mesh of wrinkles it could not smooth. The lamp in her hand was rock-steady. But her eyes were veiled. Rose knew that the dull curtain hid fear. Fear that had been a brooding threat for days, that was now a livid reality.

"Rose! Did. . . ?"

"No. I got the shutter down in time. Aunt Faith—we've got to get help. We can't stay here with—that—outside."

"Help! How?" The thin line of her mouth twisted with what might have been a bitter smile. "We dare not go—out there. And the telephone was taken out last week. They wouldn't let us have a telephone without paying for it. Our credit isn't good any more."

"Credit! But you had money. You sold the last of the silver. . . ."

"And bought food with it. Wasted it on food we'll never eat. He'll get in. . . . Rose . . . he'll find a way to get in. We can't escape him."

It wasn't so much what she said that sent chills shivering up Rose's spine; it was her tone, dull, flat, utterly hopeless. Pregnant with the same grim fatalism with which she had once said, "We must never marry. We must die friendless and alone."

"He! What—who is he? Who is the man with the horned head?" The question was wrung from her. "You know, Aunt Faith. You have been expecting this."

A muscle twitched in the sunken, age-yellowed cheek. "I? How should I know? The Lorans had many sins and many enemies. For each sin an enemy. Perhaps—a horned head! Have you forgotten your Shakespeare, child? Have you forgotten that horns on a man's forehead are the brand of a cuckold?"

A cuckold—a betrayed husband. What was the story of Uncle Roy's last escapade before the one that had ruined him? Of the girl he had met in the swamp—the wife of Gant Gorham. . . ?

Gant Gorham! Elmer's gasping, unintelligible message came back. Gant Gorham! Was it that he had tried to say? Had he been accusing the descendant of Stoddard Gorham who lived in the morass that was his inheritance, alone and half-mad in some foul shack on an island of harder ground? Rose had never seen him, but. . . .

"Aunt Faith! I can get help. I can get Walter! The roof—it's copper! I'll build a fire up there. Walter will see it. He'll come. . . ."

"No. It isn't any use. The roof isn't high enough. . . "

"It is. I've been up there and I could see his house over the trees between."

Action, any action, was a relief from dread. Rose ran into the kitchen, snatched up an armful of firewood, matches. She was out in the foyer again, was running up the great staircase, through a passage-way, up narrower steps. She wanted no light, every inch of the old house was familiar. Here was the ladder to the roof. She got the heavy trapdoor open. Wind beat in on her from the black pall of a cloud-filled sky. A storm wind. She dropped her kindling on the flat roof. Her shaking hands made a small tent of the firewood sticks. She fumbled in the little pocket of her frock for the matches.

The rustle of breeze-tossed leaves came to her, and a curious pattering like the quick beat of raindrops. But it wasn't raining yet. Rose rose to her feet, ran toward the parapet overlooking the garden. Reached it and leaned over the crumbling rail. Jagged lightning split the clouds, and the tangled brush below was vivid with blue glare.

Vivid and alive with movement. The pattering came from down there, the rapid scamper of many feet. Another lightning streamer showed. Rose knew what made it. Little animals, dozens of them, were running through the brush, running toward the house. Small black beasts. One of them was in the path. Rose gasped. It was a goat, an ebony skinned, bearded goat. But there was something grotesque about it. Something weirdly *wrong*.

Not in its shape or the manner of its pattering run. In its color. In the color of its horns and its hooves. They were not grey as a normal goat's should be. They were brightly golden. They were

gilded. . . . The beast vanished, and the beat of its weird feet came up from the porch.

She must have been mistaken. Some freak of the fitful lightning had deluded her. . . . There was another—a female. Its horns, too, gleamed, indescribably eerie.

ROSE'S hands clenched on the rail, her fingers trembling. For a moment she could not move, could not think. The murdered man, the weird pursuing figure, had already made that garden a place of fear. But it was something other than that now. It was an enclosure visited by an ancient terror, invaded by beings that were goat-form and yet were not goats. Tag ends of shivery legends slid across her pulsing brain, traditions of whispered horror. They were under her, just under her, filling the broad verandah of Loran Hall, their hoofs making a small thunder on its rotting boards. A thunder nearer than the mutter of the approaching storm.

Then there was another sound. All her life she had heard it, but in this moment it seared her with appalling dismay. The sound of creaking hinges came up to her—the creak of the great door's opening hinges. She could not be mistaken . . . .

And there were voices. Faith's harsh accents, and a bass rumble she could not recognize. . . . But it could be only the voice of Elmer's murderer!

Oh God! It had been Faith who had sent old Elmer out to his death! It had been Faith who but for her own frantic, incredible leap would have shut her out, helpless in the grip of the terror! It had been Faith who had pointed to the veiled prophecy on Pan's pedestal and laughed! Laughed in the presence of horrible death!

Faith had known of the coming of the beast and had waited for it, not with fear but with impatience. Faith had argued against the signal Rose had come up here to set, calling for help. Faith was opening the door now to let in the beast before Wally could come!

CHAPTER THREE

Man Trap

A MIST of red wrath wavered before Rose Loran's eyes. Faith Loran—Aunt Faith—had known of some awful vengeance descending on Loran Hall. To save herself she had offered Elmer as a sacrifice, and Rose. She was making that bargain now, down there, offering her niece, her ward, in exchange for her own safety. It was damnable.

The girl's small fists clenched, she whirled away from the parapet, sobbing with choked anger. They would not get away with it. She went back to the hatchway. She knelt to the fire she had laid and thrust a flaming match into the shavings at its base. The tinder caught—

A scream shrilled up from below, a high, quavering, scream exactly like Elmer's last cry from the darkness. But this was not followed by silence. It was quenched, rather, by a sudden blatting chorus of goat-cries, and by the skirling laughter of the Pan pipes.

Rose forgot her anger. She spun about, remembering only that Aunt Faith had been a mother to her, that Aunt Faith needed her now. She caught up a thick bludgeon, hurled herself down the ladder and the stairs, hurtled along the dark second floor corridor, snatched at the newel-post of the main stairway to twist herself to that last broad flight. Then she stopped, peering down, trembling. . . .

Light flickering in through the open door showed her the foyer floor. Showed her the gilt-horned goats milling around something on that floor, something twisted, and bloody, and horrible.

She saw the bronzed, naked back of a man crouched over the gory body of Aunt Faith. *If it was a man.* His hair was tight curled, shaggy. His haunches—what she could see of them—were black-furred, shaggy, bestial. His hands, spatulate, hairy, were busy with the body of the woman on the floor.

"No!" shrieked Aunt Faith. "You won't get it out of me. It's done enough damage already." Her voice was edged with terror and agony.

Rose's arm arced upward, swept down. The heavy stick flew down through the dark. She heard it crash into the creature's skull. Its thud sickened the girl, but the blow that would have dropped an ordinary man only brought a howl from the one below. He raised up, twisted about. In a new flash Rose saw the face staring up at her that had glared in through the window. The sharp-chinned, satyr's countenance. Were those horns on his brow or. . . ? Before she could make sure darkness had smashed in again with a brain-shaking peal of awesome thunder.

It seemed to come in the house and roll up the stairs beneath her. But it wasn't thunder, it was the pound of Pan's feet coming up to her. Rose whirled, leaped into a frenzied dash for safety. Where was there safety in this house invaded by terror? The roof? If she could get to the roof, fling herself over. Death, any death rather than. . . .

A hole in the frayed carpeting caught her heel, flung her down. She sprawled, despair exploding in her brain. She rolled. . . . The smell of goat flesh gusted out of the blackness. Calloused, irresistible hands gripped her shoulders. A hairy, repulsive hide was against her quivering skin. Through the thin fabric of her frock it flayed her with its roughness. . . .

A ROLLING peal of thunder died away. Lightning flashed in through the windows once more, and the electric lamp by which Walter Parton was trying to read dimmed, flared up again. He slammed his book down on the floor, unfolded his lank, loose-knit length, stood on heavy-thewed, spraddled legs. A frown creased his tanned forehead and in his brown eyes pain slept, pain that had not been long out of them through the years since Rose Loran had first told him she was not for him.

"Hell of a storm coming up," he muttered in the habit of one who is much alone. "If lightning hits that old house. . . ."

Damn it. If Rose would only get over that foolish idea of hers. If she would only let him take care of her. From that window he could just see the roof of Loran Hall. . . . About time he got over his kid habit of gazing at it for long hours, heartsick with love denied. . . . He strode across the room. . . .

He was staring out into pitch blackness. . . . What the hell! An orange spark splashed the night. It grew momentarily brighter, was unmistakably the flicker of a flame. *There was nothing over there but Rose's home!*

Parton whirled, threw himself down the stairs. He ran to the 'phone in the hall, frantically twirled its handle to call the firehouse in distant Loranton. There was no sound in the receiver slammed against his ear. No sound at all. Damnation! The rickety line was out again. Every time there was a storm it did that! Walter hurled the useless cylinder of hard rubber against the wall. He ran out of the house, leaped into the seat of his rattletrap roadster, breathing a prayer of thankfulness that he had been too lazy to garage it.

The slam of the door, the whir of the starter, the clash of gears and the roar of a hard-pushed motor merged into one continuous sound. Headlights leaped out to snatch a rushing ribbon of rutted road out of the darkness. Malformed, grotesque trees flicked by. The world lit up with a quivering blue glare of lightning and vanished again with a detonation of deafening thunder.

Underbrush scraped the flivver's sides. Boards of a narrow bridge rattled swiftly underneath. Parton's foot pounded down on the brake pedal as a great black gap in the bridge deck leaped into the glare of his headlights. The car squealed protest and the seat dropped away underneath Parton. Checked momentum slammed him forward. Windshield glass crashed. As weltering, nauseous blackness stabbed him with excruciating pain he thought he heard shrill laughter somewhere near—skirling laughter. . . .

* * *

Filthy, lecherous fingers tore at Rose Parton's clothing. A scream of nightmare horror ripped her throat.

"You devil," Faith shrieked from below. "Let her alone. I'll tell. I'll tell if you leave her."

Through retching oblivion that swept in on her Rose was vaguely conscious that the hands were no longer tearing at her. She crawled—tried to crawl. She was going down, down into nothingness.

* * *

Parton battled with unconsciousness, fought it off. Dazedly he pulled himself out from under the twisted steering wheel. Throbbing pain streaked across his cheek and the taste of his own blood was salty on his lips. An electric flicker showed him the grotesquely slanted hood of his car, the crumpled radiator crushed against a heavy board at the other side of the gap in the bridge. Painfully he got out on the running board, crept along it, dragged himself over the hood's hot metal. He was on firm ground again. He was running, running madly along a road lit only fitfully by sky-rending flashes.

And with him ran dread. For he had seen, as he struggled to get across the opening his wrecked flivver bridged, fresh scars of wood that could have been made only by an ax. That gap was not an accident of rotted timbers fallen in. It was man-made, made by someone who purposely had intended to block the road to Loran Hall.

Gasping, he reached the high iron fence around the Loran Estate. The turretted silhouette of the ancient mansion bulked against the blacker dark of the sky, and tiny flames flickered on its roof. Even as he clung, shaken and distrait, to the locked gate they were gone. Queer, he thought dully. The fire had put itself out.

And then he remembered that that roof was of copper, was impervious to flame. Remembered Rose's troubled recounting of her aunt's unaccountable fear, and the strange circumstance of the wrecked bridge. Good Lord! That fire had been a signal, a desperate call for help. The danger, whatever danger Faith Loran had feared, had descended upon Loran Hall! Rose needed him—and the fence, the locked gate, barred him out.

"Rose!" he shouted. "Rose! I'm coming. Hold on! I'm coming." He backed away, crouched. His leg-muscles uncoiled like unleashed springs, hurtled him at the barrier. His hands gripped the spikes at the top. They pierced him with new tortures. He held on, his biceps cracked, swelling, but his lifted foot groped for and found the top-rail of the fence. He was over.

He ran through the tangle of the unkept garden. A pale wraith looming above him was the statue of Pan for which Rose had taken an inexplicable dislike, right after her grandfather died. That had been part of the queer change in her that had caused him so much distress. He passed it, skidded in mud. Fell and his hand clutched into clammy flesh. He rolled away, shuddering. A lightning flash showed him horror!

He was on his feet again, reached the porch, and dashed through the door. The *open* door. Good Lord! What had happened here! What fiendish thing?

Walter Parton's mouth set into a grim line across his pallid face, as he paused, tensely listening. The musty dead smell of the ancient house was all about him. Eerie, fitful flashes of light from the lightning of the nearing storm was the only illumination in the shrouded, funereal entrance hall.

"Rose!" he shouted frantically.

Walter listened to the echoing diminuendo with which the mansion mocked him. There was no answer, but he sensed some presence here that was dread made tangible, that waited for his burning, wide-pupilled eyes to find it in the gloom. His sleeves tightened over bulging biceps, his fists knotted as if to meet an attack. And then he saw it, far back in the vague foyer; a dark mound, a motionless dark pile. He moved, stiff-legged and tensed, across the uncarpeted floor; fearing to scan the limp heap closer yet knowing that he must do so. His cold hand fumbled in a pocket, came out with a wood match as he got to the dark form. His thumb rasped across the match-head, and a little flame spurted from the splinter. Its light spilled down.

Pent breath popped from between Walter's icy lips in a choked gasp, and the match dropped from his nerveless fingers—dropped hissing into viscid liquid still oozing redly from the corpse.

CHAPTER FOUR

Clutch of the Swamp

HORROR quivered in deepening darkness, in silence thick with dread. In Walter's temples a pulse pounded against the steel band of terror that constricted his forehead, and his hand seemed mittened, clumsy as he groped for another match.

Dancing, minute light forced the lurking shadows back a little way. Queerly, even in the brutal death that had come to her, even with her skull crushed in and her thin frame contorted in final agony, something of the rigid austerity of her spinsterhood still clung to Faith Loran. But on the pallid fabric under the woman's scrawny neck, on the yellow of her skin, on the scrubbed whiteness of the wooden floor all about her, tiny footprints showed, the twin small ovals of goats' cloven hoofs stamped in thin blood! Parton caught the taint of their odor in the quivering, stifling air he pulled into his lungs. Goats! What mocking, derisive thing was this? What outer horror had invaded this old house? What incredible thing was it that had slain old Elmer and Faith? *Where was Rose?*

He shouted her name, sprang toward the stairs. His feet pounded up the great staircase, resounded through the ominous, shadowy reaches above. *"Rose!"* His shouted, frantic call echoed through emptiness. He dashed back to the entrance-hall again, staggering, grey despair masking his working face, cold sweat dripping from it. Rose was gone, was somewhere in the hands of the vicious killer. Rose was gone. . . .

Lightning framed the doorway in blue glare, vanished. It seemed to the frantic man that the inimical, haunched statue of Pan had been silhouetted right there in the opening. So real the impression was that he crouched to meet it. A foul, animal-like odor engulfed him, and a hard fist crashed against his shoulder. With appalling suddenness Parton was involved in a maelstrom of fierce combat, was fighting for his life with an eerily huge antagonist who had about him some

macaber weirdness that made Walter's blood run cold within him even as he fought.

The smash of hairy fists, impacting on his bones as though the cushion of his flesh and muscle had been stripped away, pounded excruciating agony through him. Walter sidestepped, got home with his own fist, might veritably have been battling the stone monument for all the effect it had. His adversary was gigantic, seemed possessed of supernormal strength and gave vent to grunting, animal sounds that tightened its unearthly, terror-inspiring quality. Parton rained futile blows on the monstrous thing that sought his destruction. Skinned knuckles were the reward of his efforts, and pain that shot up his arms, paralyzed his muscles.

The thing that had come out of the night closed in; relentless, implacable. Parton felt shaggy arms wrap around his weakening body, and he was hugged tight to a steel-hard torso. The bands that clamped him constricted, drove the breath from his chest. He felt his ribs caving in, his tortured spine cracking. His eyes bulged, he tasted the salt of blood on his lips. . . .

THE world exploded in a tremendous blast that swallowed Loran Hall in a coruscation of electricity gone mad! Flame spurted—was it in his own head? Walter carommed into a corner, slammed against a papered wall. He slid to the floor. He knew that the gargoylesque shape whose attack had so nearly destroyed him had rushed to the back of the house, had disappeared.

Acrid smoke stung his nostrils.

Afterwards Walter wondered that he was able to force himself to his feet, to reel after his late antagonist. It was the thought of Rose that spurred him past the stairs, through the wavering flames of the fire the lightning-flash had set—the thought that this being would lead him to Rose.

A blank wall confronted Parton, but to his right there was a door. He whirled to it, flung it open. Lurid firelight flared in, lit up wooden, descending steps. Walter threw himself down those steps, saw a stone-vaulted basement receding into shadow, heard a grating noise and the faint echo of a taunting laugh.

Fire-glare set his long shadow dancing on tamped-down earth that showed no trace of any passing. Lightning flicked through a high-up small window, revealed the cellar from end to end, from side to side. It was starkly empty. Cobwebs hung undisturbed from beamed rafters, the dust of years was clotted on grimly grey foundation stones that were its walls.

A racking cough seized Walter, doubled him up with its paroxysm. His eyes were streaming, misted. He was aware that smoke was pouring down the stairs behind him, heard the crackle of flames. He twisted about, saw red firelight darting ominously through a billowing smoke-cloud. He was caught by the fire, caught down here to be cremated in a raging furnace, to end with the end of Loran Hall. . . .

Heat beat on Walter Parton's back like the breath of a Moloch. Flames hissed, then roared hungrily as old wood caught and blazed. Jagged fingers, yellow and orange and oddly green, reached for him out of the rolling murk, snatched at him hungrily. Impossible to return up those fiery stairs—and there was no other way out of this basement. He was cut off, doomed!

Parton groaned, dropped, crawled along the earthen cellar-floor on hands and knees, his head low to seek what little clearer air there was down here. Strength seeped from him. He couldn't breathe. Suffocation would claim him in minutes now. At least he would be unconscious when the raging flames reached him.

His head struck stone, rough stone of the farther wall. Walter lay still, gasping, despair a leaden weight at his stomach-pit.

The smoke lifted over him, seemed to be drawn upward so as to give him a slightly greater space of comparatively clean air to breathe. It was being drawn upward! He could see the curl of the tendrils, their ascending current, remembered the high-placed window. Luck, or some guiding Providence, had brought him just beneath it. But that window was ten feet above him; beyond his reach and, perhaps, too small to permit his passage.

Parton filled his lungs, scrambled to his feet. His clawing fingers found chinks in the masonry, his toes scraped, caught in tiny interstices. He climbed painfully up the rough wall. His hand found the window-sill, agonizing effort got his knees onto the narrow ledge.

A chink between sash and frame gave him time for another breath, but it was smoke-tainted, cut his chest with its knife-edge stab. A cough tore at his throat. He fought it, fearful that it might jar him from his frail hold. He felt grimy glass, smashed it, felt the shards cut his fists but did not feel the pain.

The opening pulled smoke, heat, over and around him. Walter shoved his head through, but his shoulders caught. He squirmed. Jagged glass ripped his shirt, his flesh. The taper of his frame to the waist made passage easier when his shoulders were through and he was out, was sprawling in dry grass. The fire roared like a dissappointed demon, and almost continous thunder answered it.

PARTON staggered erect. The weed-grown grounds were luminous with the blue flicker of lightning and the red glare of the blazing house. He sought the statue of Pan. It was in its accustomed place. But it seemed to have turned on its pedestal to face him, and its grin to have become a smirk of evil, leering triumph.

The heavens burst into electric flame. Cataclysmic sound shook the earth. Beyond Pan a dark figure moved, raised itself over the fence. vanished into the encroaching woods. How had he gotten out of the basement and across the grounds? Parton shuddered. There was something ungodly about the distorted creature.

The iron fence was too high for him to climb in his weakness. Memory came to his aid, he found a depression that had served him long ago, wriggled under the barrier.

Thick-knit leaf-ceiling overhead quenched lightning-flicker; intervening trunks blocked the glare of the fire and impenetrable gloom swallowed him. But there was the threshing of a heavy body ahead for him to follow, the dull thudding of footfalls unnaturally ponderous.

The footing grew soft. Moisture-drenched soil sucked at Parton's heels. He was, he realized, on the edge of Gorham's Swamp. That was where the thing ahead of him was going. The lay of land here, the playground of his boyhood, was familiar to him as the palm of his hand. The guiding sounds had vanished but he didn't need them any longer. There was only one way into the morass. Foot-wide, masked by cattails and rushes, a single causeway of solid earth meandered across the bog, widening to make the island where Gant Gorham's shanty stood.

Gant Gorham! Enlightenment burst on Parton. Gant Gorham, implacable enemy of the Lorans, was behind this, although the monstrous shape that had lurched in through the Hall's doorway at him was not that of the swamp-dweller.

Furtive sounds behind him, a strange sensation of inimical eyes watching, prickled the nape of his neck with fear. Parton whirled. Nothing was there. Nothing but the silent, gloom-shrouded forest, the distorted bulks of malformed trees.

Overcast, black sky came again into view as the woods thinned at the bleak edge of the swamp. Here was the cairn of stones that he had helped to erect as a boy, to mark the entrance of the natural causeway. It lay ahead, tortuous, but his feet remembered every twisted curve of it.

WALTER was tight-faced as he set out on the dangerous passage, his eyelids narrowed to thread-like slits, muscle-ridges lumping along his blunt jaw. Rose was on that island just ahead, and the swart-visaged killer who had stolen her for some mad purpose of a twisted mind. Gorham was there. . . . Walter swore between white lips that neither Gorham nor the devil himself could stand between him and the girl he loved.

The swamp was not silent, things slithered through it—ominous things of slime and scum. A bubble plopped in thick mud, and a small creature shrieked as quicksand caught it. Walter was in the center of the morass, moving cautiously despite his haste, drawing on memory for the path he must tread to avoid foul death waiting on either side.

The shrilly liquid skirling of pipes laughed behind him, changed quickly to goat-call. Wally started to run, twisted back as the quick patter of tiny hooves came to him from the island ahead. Black against black, a small form rushed out on the causeway. Another. Lightning lit up the world and Parton saw that the narrow path was alive with black-skinned goats, with a shoving, pell-mell rush of ruminants whose hooves and horns were gilded. The weird sight struck a sudden, queasy terror into Parton, filled him with a sense that powers other than human were battling against him for the body and the soul of the girl he loved.

The pipes called again, blurring, shrieking with a queer madness. Maddened bleating answered. The grotesquely ornamented goats, crazed by the Hamelin piping, stampeded toward him. They piled up, shoving one another from the causeway, screaming with almost human agony as the black mud and the quicksand caught them, screaming till their shrieks blubbed into silence.

Ten, a dozen of the onrushing small animals were thrust to muddy death, but the others came on as the skirling of the Pan-pipes crescendoed. They came on, an irresistible avalanche of gilt-horned destruction that must surely throw him from the path, into the slow, strangling death of the quicksand.

He could not stop them, no power on earth could stop them. Man or devil he would have fought on that precarious footing, would have fought and flung into the quaking bog, but these horned creatures, these miniature incarnations of a world gone insane, he was powerless against.

He turned to run, to give them passage and return after they had passed—and recoiled as a gargoylesque dark mass hurtled toward him from the swamp-edge whence he had just come. The thing that had attacked him in the old house was plunging along the path. Its grotesque, gigantic goat-shape was more noisome than the swamp; its shaggy arms flailing against the tempest-lit sky were like fungus-coated limbs of a dead tree come to unholy life.

Walter's lips grimaced in a snarl of hate, and he lunged to meet the weird attack. But the momentary halt was fatal. Horns, a hard head, catapulted into him from behind, battered him from the causeway. He arced through muggy air, sprawled into black mud that geysered as his frame splashed into it. Mud slapped across his face, blinded him, thrust its stinking mush into his nostrils, his mouth, his ears. Instinct pulled his head up and back, out of the half-liquid slime. Instinct betrayed him as the movement drove his legs down and the sliding, granular mass of quicksand clamped his feet and ankles. He was trapped, caught in the quicksand, and terror tore at his throat.

Above him Pan-pipes laughed gloatingly. The woods, cowering beneath the impending onslaught of the gale, caught up the laughter and tossed it from contorted bole to writhing limb. Slime-born things slithered close around him, and clammy coldness whipped across his hand.

The pipes laughed again, their laughter trilled into goat cry. The hairy little things that had encompassed his destruction—those that remained—wheeled and scampered back to the island, vanished. More slowly the piper lurched after them.

Between Walter and the island an enmeshed goat screamed in agony. Its scream was poignant, human. Again the quivering sound came. But this time it was not a goat that screamed. It was a woman. It was Rose!

Rose was screaming in terror as the goat-man followed his creatures into islet's mystery, and Parton only yards away, could not help her. The quicksand ran away from beneath his feet like the slow, inevitable ebbing of grains in an hourglass measuring the short space of life left to him. Surface slime already chilled his calves, lapped slowly higher.

Rose's scream stopped short, as if a hairy palm had thudded across her mouth. And the Pan-pipes laughed on the island, trilled obscene glee as jelled mud quivered slowly upward to the trapped man's slim waist.

CHAPTER FIVE

The End of the Lorans

JAGGED blue split the universe from horizon to horizon, and the riven cosmos crashed together again with devastating sound.

The encompassing cloud opened and belched its contents. The air was suddenly solid with the cataract, the earth flattened by the downpour. Walter's world was the inexorable clutch of mud and sand about his legs, his waist, his abdomen. His body throbbed with pain and despair.

If only, he thought, that lightning had struck the island and killed Rose, he could die content. Perhaps it had—God grant that it had.

Water swirled about his chest and his neck, boiled over his tight lips; water lashed to foam by more water that descended in flooding torrents.

In seconds now it would be over his nostrils, and that would be the end. Rose. . . .

The slow creep of the quicksand was halted. The lift of the two-foot layer of new water covering the swamp was sufficient to balance its sucking.

But that water would drown him. It was a cleaner death, but death nevertheless. Why not duck his head the inch it would take to meet that death?

Something bumped against him. His finger clutched shaggy hair, horns scraped his side.

It was a goat, and the creature was moving, moving strongly. The water that had been sufficient only to keep Parton from sinking had pulled the animal's slim legs free of the mud, and the goat was half-swimming, half-running parallel to the causeway.

Walter reached for the ruminant's horns. The goat's forelegs found firmer ground almost at once. It bleated, surged strongly ahead. That surge was just sufficient to pull Walter free of the mire, to drag him, too, to where he could find firm enough foothold for the final effort

that released him from the bog's lethal grip.

Ahead of him was a rain-lashed clearing; but from somewhere came a faint glimmer, and Walter Parton could see the herd of goats huddled against unpainted boards of Gorham's shack. Above them a thin right-angle of yellow light came from within, otherwise cut off by some covering that blanketed the window.

Parton knew he must get to that window, must peer through it. But the goats were right there, their scattering would betray his presence. Already they were restless, bleating.

A door creaked open on the other side of the shack. Small heads tossed, a billy blatted. The herd wheeled, crashed into the woods.

Parton lay close to the muddy, stinking ground waiting for discovery. But the hidden door shut again, and no threatening form loomed around the corner of the decrepit hut. Parton squirmed to it, raised himself to the window.

The slit that was the only aperture for his spying was threadlike, and a little way from it, within, something blocked Walter's vision.

He moved a bit, brought into sight a recumbent head, an unshaven, brutal mustached countenance beneath whose leathery skin death-pallor showed. Wally's forehead knitted. This was Gorham, Gant Gorham. But the man was unconscious or dead. Who then. . . ?

Someone moaned within, moaned with hopeless pain. Walter's scalp tightened. That whimper of agony came from Rose's throat, or he had never heard her voice. His decision was made in an instant. He turned about to get to the door of the shack. . . . Something crashed against the back of his neck, against his head, and oblivion swept over his senses.

"I TELL you I don't know," Rose was screaming. "I don't know and I can't tell you."

Her agonized voice pulled Walter out of the pain and the darkness in which he weltered, pulled him up to the throbbing torture of torn body, and nerves. His eyes opened. . . .

Gant Gorham lay motionless on a pallet of rags just under the window that was blinded by a tattered quilt. Lamplight flickered across his face, giving it a semblance of life, but the black hilt of a knife protruded from his bloody chest. A twisted man-creature crouched, blocking Wally's further view. It moved. . . .

Rose hung against the wall, her wrists bound by rope to rusted spikes dirven deep into the wood, her arms straight lines of tensed anguish. Her chestnut hair framed a face that was strained and lined with suffering. Her body writhed—its clean sun-browned curves naked except for a lacy wisp pendent between waist and thighs. Muscles across her drawn-in abdomen pulsed, and the strained lines of her arms were repeated in the terrific straining of her legs as her toetips touched the grimy floor.

Parton pulled silently at ropes that were tight around his ankles, that bound his arms to his flanks. His efforts were futile. An expert hand had knotted them, the hair-covered, long-nailed hand hanging now beside a shaggy, curiously formed haunch. That hand opened and closed as Parton watched it. Every line of its grotesque owner betrayed evil malevolence incarnate.

The rasping, hoarse voice that answered the girl's defiance was as animal-like, as weirdly bestial as his macaber form. "You know, damn you. You know where Faith hid the Loran treasure. She opened the door to beg me to go away and then she fooled me, the devil take her rotten soul. There wasn't anything under the Pan statue. If I hadn't killed her I would have made her tell what she did with it; but I'll get it out of you if I have to strip every inch of skin from your cursed body." His other arm jerked into Walter's vision, swishing. It was a whip that swished, a thick whip of corded snake-skin. The cruel lash whistled, cracked across the girl's taut abdomen. A livid weal oozed blood. . . .

Walter rolled, thumped against the hairy legs of the torturer. The monster staggered. Parton managed to squirm his legs about those hairy ones and the gigantic form collapsed upon him. It jolted over. Thick, hard thumbs closed on the bound man's throat, dug in. Walter's breath was cut off. His eyes were bulging. Darkness, the darkness of death, swirled about him. . . .

"Don't Uncle Roy," Rose screamed. "Don't."

Her own fierce pains were forgotten as she stared at the terrible thing on the floor, as she saw Walter's tortured face turn purple, then blacken. . . . And then new horror swamped her as the dead man on the pallet moved. Incredibly he was rising from the cot. . . .

The corpse's grimy hand jerked up with a horrible, mechanical motion, closed on the knife-handle jutting from his chest. A spurt of clotted blood followed the blade as he pulled it out. The dagger arced through the air, plunged into the back of the murderer. Gorham collapsed on top of the man he had come back from death to kill, and Walter was drowned in the spate of scarlet blood gushing over him from both writhing forms.

THE storm was over, and a pallid moon looked down on two half-naked figures, a man's and a girl's, that staggered out of the woods cloaking Gorham's Swamp.

"Gorham wasn't dead, then," Walter

muttered. "The knife kept the wound it had made closed, and he wasn't dead."

"He was probably conscious for a long time, waiting for the chance you gave him. Oh, Walter, you were so brave. . . ."

"Never mind that. . . . Here, we can crawl under the fence right here. . . . You called that—that *thing* Uncle Roy."

"He was Uncle Roy, the man we all thought dead. Do you remember in the newspaper account of the fight in which he was supposed to have been killed it spoke of another one who was badly wounded and taken to the hospital unconscious?"

"Yes."

"That was Roy Loran. He told me all about it while he carried me through the swamp after he heard you shouting out by the gate. But he might as well have been dead, for years. One bullet chipped his skull, depressed a bit of bone that pressed into his brain and wiped out his memory. He was sent to an institution, escaped, and found work somewhere not far from here as a goat-herd.

"Then he had another accident, and he recalled who he was. He wrote to Aunt Faith, about a month ago, telling her all this and demanding a great deal of money to remain unknown. She replied to tell him there was no money and he answered that he knew the first Loran had a fortune hidden somewhere on the ground, that he was coming to wring the secret out of her lying throat.

"She didn't tell me a word of this, hoping he was bluffing, but he did come. What he suspected was true enough. Faith knew of the hiding place, in a tunnel from the basement of the Hall to an exit under the Pan statue. . . ."

"The devil!" Wally interrupted. "That was why he ran when the lightning struck. He was afraid the fire would block him from it."

"Aunt Faith told him the secret to save me from him. Then he heard your shout and carried me off to the hut in the swamp. Gorham came in, went for him, and he stabbed him. . . .

"He went out again, probably to look in the tunnel for the treasure. The blatting of the goats drove me mad. . . ."

"The goats! What on earth. . . ."

"I imagine his darkened mind must have retained some memory of the Pan statue. He had painted their horns and their hooves and trained them to answer his piping. When he returned he brought his herd along."

Wally shuddered, held Rose close to him. "Somehow they were the worst of the whole business. There was something incredibly evil about them."

"Terribly! They were like little imps from hell itself. . . . I was frantic, bound there, alone, not knowing what to expect. And then, when the storm broke, he burst in, frothing at the mouth and raving that Faith and I had robbed the cache and hidden the treasure somewhere else. He hung me up as I was when you found me, swearing that he would torture me till I told him where it was. I—"

"Don't talk about it any more sweetheart. It's all done for, finished. The Lorans are finished—"

Rose smiled demurely. "You forget, Wally, that I am a Loran."

"We'll change that as soon as we get to the Reverend Wilkin's house," Walter grinned. "Rose Parton is a much better name."

Loran Hall was a mass of charred timbers, of black, drenched coals. But Pan was still on his pedestal, and the moon seemed to touch the inscription with a ghostly, meaningful hand.

The lovers paused briefly to read it. Rose sighed through her tears. "The Lorans have paid the piper, all right, for all their dances. There are no more Lorans."

THE END